John Bartlett Wicks

My Bird Parishioners

St. Paul's parish, Paris Hill, N.Y., 1897

John Bartlett Wicks

My Bird Parishioners
St. Paul's parish, Paris Hill, N.Y., 1897

ISBN/EAN: 9783337328535

Printed in Europe, USA, Canada, Australia, Japan

Cover: Foto ©Andreas Hilbeck / pixelio.de

More available books at **www.hansebooks.com**

My
Bird
Parishioners.

St. Paul's Parish,
Paris Hill, N. Y.

1897.

" The sparrow hath found her an house, and
the swallow a nest, where she may lay her
young; even thy altars, O Lord of hosts, my
King and my God."—*Psalm 84 : 3.*

TO OLD ST. PAUL'S CHURCH, PARIS HILL, VEN-
ERABLE WITH YEARS, AND HOLY WITH SA-
CRED MEMORIES, THIS LITTLE BOOKLET
IS DEDICATED, AS A TOKEN OF THE
AUTHOR'S AFFECTION FOR THE
CHURCH OF HIS BOYHOOD,
AND OF SO MANY
OF HIS RIPER
YEARS.

—J. B. Wicks.

T IS one thing to be an ornithologist, and another to be a companion and lover of birds. Probably my friend, the Pastor on Paris Hill, does not so much concern himself with the scientific structure, anatomy or nomenclature of his subject, in the *Genus* and *Species*, with organization or classification, whatever his knowledge of those matters may be, as with the living, flying, singing creature in the air, or the grass, or the nest, or on the tree, the bush, or the barn. He deals, that is, with his parishioners in the forest and field, as he does with his parishioners in the church; he takes them, watches them, studies them, alive. In each of the congregations he finds songs and songsters; who shall say he does not find worshippers? If he preaches to the winged things, he does only what the great Saint Francis of Assisi did, and doubtless does it as well. He has been familiar with both audiences from his babyhood, and who can wonder that mutual confidence and sympathy have grown up between them?

Apart from the charm, the instruction and the in-
genuity of this book itself, those who read it—and
they should be many—may learn from it how much
more the world of nature about us has to give us
than most of us are apt to take or seek, what stores
of satisfying knowledge and rich delight lie close at
hand, and how true it is that what we really see day
by day depends less on the objects and scenes before
our eyes than on the eyes themselves and the minds
and hearts that use them.

F. D. HUNTINGTON.

Syracuse, Nov. 29, 1896.

THE COMING OF THE BIRDS.

I.

PARIS HILL, with all its disadvantages, is Scriptural in its location, having its commanding place where it can not be hid. Some of the early settlers, we know, found their way to this range of hills and took up their claims here because it was hill country. High as the snow may pile, it never buries the hill out of sight, and never in its passing floods the roads and farms, or carries away the bridges that span the rivulets which run among the hills. The winter of 1895-6, like its predecessors, has been prolific in wind and cold, and, unlike some of them, has flung the snow far and wide, even shaping it into huge drifts that from a little distance can easily be mistaken for the sand dunes of the seashore. Several months of this piling and shaping easily gives the snow hills not only place but character. In our little village during the past winter the architect and builder of the white drifts has been the west wind. The other breezes have simply played a little here and there, but with

no perceptible influence.   From the west towards the
east the palaces of glistening crystal have risen slowly
until they seem a part of the hamlet itself.

Out into the park, from the open space south of
Graham's store, is the drift easily first among the
many.   Below it, on the same side of the village, are
its fellows, like the outlying bastions of some great
fort, leading one to think that the wind shapes all its
creations after some well-considered design.,   The
curious feature, however, is the fact that each drift
folds itself about house and church as though its
mission was to keep and defend.   The Congrega-
tional session room is buttressed far up above the
door, and to seek its cozy aisles is to press through
the narrow, if not straight, way.   It may be fancy,
but to me there is the Frost-King, ruling in the
realm of snow and ice, sending out his frost and cold,
blowing with his great winds and building his houses
that glisten in the sunlight, like the fabled creations
of the Arabian Nights.   All of it to the devout soul is
redolent with the sentiment of the old hymn :
"Bless ye the Lord! Praise Him and magnify Him
forever !"

But the day of the snow passes, and the spring
time is given place.   Our first day of real freedom
came the 30th of March.   In the early morning the
sky was lighted by a few flashes of electricity, and a

little later the first birds told the story we had all
been waiting so long to hear. The clear note of the
robin welcomed the rising sun. No other birds appeared, but it was all the same to robin.
He went on cheerily, doing his best. What
a brusque fellow he is! How the spring air,
or something else, seems to thrill every nerve
in robin's body with new, stirring life! It may be
he has some idea of the work that lies before him
and prepares for it in a few days of wild, rollicking
fun. Several of them have looked in upon me to-
day. They all come with a whirring rush, ringing
out their sharp note and jerking their little bodies
as though life was all to be lived in a moment. If
there were only some way of interviewing the dap-
per fellows what stories of adventure they would un-
fold! I remember seeing a company of these birds
spending the winter in the far southwest. They had
laid aside all the domestic quietness which marks
their summer demeanor at the north, and roamed
about as happy as a company of school boys out for
a long vacation. In the entire year robin devotes
but two or three months to housekeeping. During
that time he is a changed being. Just the day it is
all settled how and where to begin the summer work,
the free-lance character disappears and the pair,
newly mated, take up the sober duties of life. All

the birds are of one kin in this, and so seem not
very far removed from their brethren of nature human.

Just a day later than the robins, the meadow-
larks and bluebirds appeared, and on the next day
the sparrows came trooping in. Some of the details
of this annual migration of the birds we know, but
the hidden part is vastly larger than the part revealed. They go from us—myriads of them,—and
almost all we know of it is the void they leave behind. They come again, as they are now coming,
and we hardly know more of their coming than that
they have come. The night closes in upon us clear,
with the snow rapidly melting—not a bird in sight
or sound. The morning dawns, and the dwellers of
an entire county are saluted with the matins of
legions of the feathered songsters. There is reason
for believing that the great host is marshalled with
some regard for order. They come with the effi-
ciency and precision of a well-ordered army. Apparently they occupy several degrees of latitude at one
stroke, and when once they have taken possession,
in some way, they seem quite oblivious to everything
but just the cheer of living. For days they go to
and fro, seemingly the freest among the free; but
all the time the spirit of business is inciting them.
The free movement, the rapid flight, and the stirring

notes, are strains of the nuptial song that eventually domiciles an unnumbered host of merry housekeepers in all our groves and fields.   How little of
this great hive of song and work, of cheeriest, sweetest life we ever see.   All the year, from the earliest
spring time to the coming of the snow in the fall,
this wealth of bird-life is in our very midst.   It is
the open book of our wide hills and vales, and it is
the purpose of the writer of this article, from time to
time, to turn the pages of this book that all may see
and enjoy with him the story of the freest, merriest
dwellers of our favored land.

II.

Snow and cold have given quite a chill to our April air. The birds have made a note of the fact and apparently fitted their song to the changed conditions. The soberer notes, however, have the ring of spring life in them, and to the ear that is really open to Mother Nature's sounds, are full of the richest music. One of our winter denizens —and summer denizens too—never seems to make any difference in the song he sings ; that is, it always appears to have about the same amount of cheer in it. Perhaps that is a part of the reason why one of our most prominent localities has been named after this bird of black—"Crow Hill." By the way, I learn from articles published, that this same Crow Hill is to become the summer home of some of our Utica friends. The writer has known the locality from boyhood and can testify to its attractions. For a summer home it can not be excelled. The view in any direction to the north and west, is simply magnificent. The strange thing about it is that it has not been sought as a summer resort long ere this.

It is the northern spur of the range of hills which extend to the southward and culminate in Tassel Hill, near Waterville, the highest point in southern Oneida. A mile to the southeast of Crow Hill is a prominent point known as Smith Hill. In part, it overlooks the former, and fairly rivals it in its wide sweep of vision. It commands the same broad expanse of the Mohawk valley and of the western hills, with a more extensive view of the high country beyond Sauquoit. It is a well wooded summit, with some fine springs along its western slope. Chadwicks, on the D., L. & W., lies almost under its eastern side, two miles away. Still farther to the south is a hill somewhat lower, that has long been noted for its extremely fine view. Captain John Wicks, one of Paris' pioneers, found this spot to his liking and for many years made it justly celebrated for his courtly sailor hospitality. Southward from this point, along both slopes of the range, the outlook varies as the hills bend outward into the valley or shrink away into the heart of the range.

Just at the foot of Tassel Hill, a few hundred yards from the Paris station, Mr. Russell H. Wicks, of Utica, has his summer cottage. It stands in a maple grove looking toward the sunrise. Its view among the hills of the range cannot be surpassed. Not far away in the years, the writer fancies, the electrics will

spin along this elevated plateau, and cottages will be
dropped here and there over the entire slope.   The
Massachusetts' cities have utilized their surroundings
in this way, notably Pittsfield, Springfield and Wor-
cester, and have found by experience that it is
the most satisfactory and inexpensive way of securing
a summer outing.   Of course the lake scenery and its
pastime of boating and fishing are wanting in this
Paris-Berkshire ; but on the other hand the little ones
may ramble and play far and near, and the fond
mothers have no concern regarding their entire safety
from all peril of cliff or of pond.   The summer
breezes of the Paris hills are famous for their invigor-
ating healthfulness, and the streams that find their
way down the sloping sides sparkle in the sunlight—
the best " free silver coinage " the writer knows.

Cradled on the very summit of the range, east of
Paris village a little distance, lies a marshy tract covered more or less densely with pine, fir and cedar
growth. Undoubtedly in some eon far away a beautiful sheet of water, like the crescent moon, reached out
and clasped the village site in its sparkling embrace.
Prof. Root, of Hamilton college,—the first bearing
that honored name in those classic halls—explored
all the recesses of the hill swamp. It was an experience of the writer's boyhood to accompany the pro-
fessor on several expeditions, and to have often

heard him say that " there was no place in the wide range of his knowledge that grew such a great variety of plants as the Paris swamp." In its deeper recesses is found the white cyprepedium, the moccasin flower or lady-slipper of the country side. I think he told me he found this flower nowhere else in this part of the state. The writer has never seen it in any other locality. Last summer our closest researches only revealed two or three specimens. Several other flowers of the orchid family are found here, also the pitcher plant, and just at the edge of the hard land the " Indian Pipe." The bird life is varied, as it is in all this region. The one song of the Hermit Thrush, however, is the unrivaled melody of these leafy aisles. Mr. Burroughs is surely interpreting nature rightly when he says: " The song of the Hermit Thrush is the spiritual song among the birds." The old Moyer road intersects the swamp on its southern border, or rather finds its way through where a narrow neck of hard land extends nearly across the marsh. Tradition says that a division of General Sullivan's army passed over this point, and that some of the logs with which he bridged the low ground are yet sound and intact, forming the foundation of the road bed. Before the whites came the road was the Indian trail from the Mohawk below Utica, directly through to Oneida lake.

Farther over on the eastern slope, north of what is now known as the Frederick Simmons' farm, there is a wide sweep of hillside mostly wooded, that reaches to the vicinity of Smith's Hill above noted. This extensive tract is seamed with deep ravines which open down into the Sauquoit valley, each the home of an old time trout brook. The writer well remembers when the virgin-forest covered all this region with a timber growth that betokens the richest of soils, as well as the favorite home of the wild birds and animals. The animals have mostly disappeared, but the birds still find their way to this favored spot, in great numbers. The spring carpet is so spangled with wild flowers that it seems the reflection of the brilliant plumage of the songsters flashing through the trees. Here a little later we shall find the thrushes, warblers, indigo birds, rose breasted grossbeaks and many others. In this connection it is curious how the birds seem to arrange for their summer campaign. Feathered neighborliness is with rule and without rule. In the open fields, the species keep to their appointed places and I judge this plan obtains in the woods. If a family of robins nest in my yard there may be several nests of other species, but no more robins on that acre. Part of the reason for this undoubtedly is the fact that families of different species use different food. The same pasture presents the variety and the birds know how to take advantage of it. Birds of long flight, like the wild pigeon, can easily nest together and seek their food over an entire state. All birds nest at the when and where of a plentiful supply of food for their young. This time would seem to be the bright summer tide, in every case ; but there are birds which build their nests and rear their young in midwinter.

One of the family of finches which some times pays us a visit, nests in the northern forests in the winter. It finds the food for its young nicely stored in the great trees, and never fails of having a large supply. On the morning of April 9, the grackle and song-sparrow made their first bow in my yard, and seemed so perfectly at home that I could hardly realize that six months had passed since our last interview. Mr. Grackle threw down the gauntlet to Mr. Robin, and was met half way, just as they saluted each other a year ago. The story of the battle and the outcome will find its place in another paper.

III.

A bright, sunny morning full of April cheer, easily led my steps to the large wood and swamp just east of Paris Hill. A sharp frost the previous night had macadamized the deep snow that lay like a carpet over the entire ground, and I found no difficulty in threading the leafy aisles with ease and comfort. The early comers among the birds find this thicket of evergreen to their liking. Just at the door of the wood, the slope down from the village was alive with robins. As far as I could trace the bare surface skirting the swamp-side, the birds were flying, running, and uttering their sharp call as though all their welfare hung upon the moments then passing. There were hundreds of them, and nearly all that I saw were male birds. Perhaps part of the activity under my eye was the offspring of the joy that dwells in all hearts in the spring time, and part the ebb and flow of the tide of life that in a few days would dot all the land with happy robin homes. Seated on the old worm fence that I had known from boyhood, I tried for a little time to catch the import of robin's call. If I understood it at all there was a sharp, quick word of wild joy and another of alarm that varied slightly from the former. Then a rattling fire of sounds that seemed at times a challenge to bat- tle, or a call to competition in a short, rapid flight. On the topmost bough of the tree near by one was pouring forth the notes of a full song, which curious- ly enough is interpreted in various ways, sometimes termed the rain song and again the greeting of the morning, or the salutation to the mate. At this particular time I fancied that a little of the music was in honor of the guest, all uninvited, but appre- ciated. Suddenly, as though all were animated by one spirit, the entire flock, with voices high pitched, scurried away to a bold point beyond the southern trend of the swamp. On from my fence seat, the way was over the high snow-banks that the west wind had sifted among the cedars Hard and firm, the path in any direction was almost in the tops of the trees. Descending toward the heart of the denser growth, I left the drifts behind, and found the carpet of white almost a yard in thickness over the entire surface. Here there was a hearty hand shake ex- tended to me by the chickadees and wood-peckers. The former are always ready with their greeting. Al- most always—winter and summer alike—a little bevy of half a dozen, more or less, will meet me at the

very door of the wood, and, though my stroll be long
or short, they keep within sound and are the very
last of the forest dwellers to say good-bye.

What busy fellows they are, scarcely ever still for
a moment. I have a notion that they are adepts in
mingling play and work. Just at the far border of
the swamp I discovered the home of a pair of chickadees. A little above my reach they had bored into
a convenient tree, and were ready for the summer
house-keeping. The woodpeckers and chickadees
stay with us through the winter. Their storehouse
of food is very nicely arranged for them. I opened
the door of one in an open reach of the swamp and
found it well stocked, though its supply had been
drawn upon extensively. Curious how Mother Nature cares for her children. Here was a tamarack
that in its dead and half decayed state was occupied
by a large number of insects. Snugly folded away
beneath the bark and in the wood, they waited the
touch of the summer breezes to spring into a new
and richer life. The birds had gone up and down the
slender boll of the tree, and only here and there had
a dweller escaped them. Whether there is any chance
here for the survival of the fittest among the insects,
I have no means of telling.

A little farther on I came upon the winter road of
the lumberman, and the opening here and there told

of many a fine tree missing. I know the wants of man demand the trees, and that they must be supplied, but I do not enjoy the disfiguring of the familiar wood-haunts, and I fancy my friends, the birds and animals, do not like it. In one of the little clearings the crows were holding a council—a political convention it may have been for aught I know. At all events it was a wordy time in crow parlance. "All at once," seemed to be the rule governing the speakers, and "Loud and long" was another rule equally prominent. So intent were they concerning their special business, that contrary to the usual way, I was almost in the open space before they knew of my approach. The instant, however, of the discovery every crow was in motion with voice and wings. Not one stayed upon the " order of his going," and I soon had the hall of the woods left entirely to my use.

One of the trees that had been cut away was associated with an experience of mine some years ago. I had discovered a hawk's nest snugly located in the thickest part of the tree, and a short acquaintance with the old birds uncovered peculiarities of character well worth noting. I was sitting near the nest one day watching the family so busy with home duties that I received not so much as a gleam of notice. The mother bird was feeding and caressing the young ones, and for an hour or more the male bird had not

been in sight. A little company of crows were foraging in an open pasture on the old Moshier hillside.
I heard them calling to each other, and soon the
heavy flapping of wings announced their presence at
the very door of our hawk's humble abode. One
sable fellow carelessly blundered right into the nest.
He had hardly touched it, however, when the male
bird, with a sharp cry, darted forth from his hidden
lookout, and at the first stroke tumbled the frightened crow fairly to the ground. The second stroke
followed the first so quickly that the poor crow had
time only to trundle away into the bushes, harrassed
at every turn by the angry hawk. The hurried
movement and awkward cries of the thoroughly
frightened crow formed a most ludicrous scene, and
I fancied that the crow spectators rather enjoyed
their fellow's discomfiture.

Finding my way along the wood road I came to
the open side of the swamp, all nicely screened from
the cool wind and flooded with the morning sunshine. The song sparrows had gathered here in
great numbers. Every bush held one or more, and,
of course, every bush was bubbling over with music.
Occasionally I caught the plaintive note of the wood-
pewee, but the concert was almost entirely sparrows'
own. I could detect three or four kinds, but the
field or vesper sparrow predominated. Among the

notes of the open fields vesper has the honor of shaping the first and best. Like all other music, however, it is at its best when in its home place. In an old hillside pasture, just as the day closes, one gets the vesper song, clear, full, and at its sweetest strain. Sometimes a dozen singers will vie together as though it were their large duty to welcome the advent of darkness. I have heard the song when the darkness was too dense to discover the singer.

Vesper is identified by the place he makes his home, as readily as by his song. After the season is fairly open he is found almost entirely in the fields. Another index to his species is the two white lateral tail feathers conspicuously displayed as he flies directly from one. The nest is usually tucked away in some convenient bank or a cavity hollowed in a rich meadow sward. The coarser grass serves for the framework, but the lining is of finer threads which the birds weave into shape with skill and dispatch. I know of no sound more quietly domestic than the sweet song of the vesper sparrow, just as the summer day is softly folded into night. One can easily fancy it the tender soul greeting of the spirit of the day, sung to the merry nymphs that sport and joy in the gloaming.

IV.

There is reason for believing that the birds are unusually numerous this season. Several kinds have shown their numbers largely beyond any year that I now remember. It may be that the supply of food is larger. More food, more birds. The earth worms in lawn and garden are most abundant and some kinds of insects' eggs, I notice, are plentiful. Robins, sparrows, larks and woodpeckers feast on the worms and insects, and are the kinds which swarm in our fields and groves. The common bluebird hardly seems represented. I have seen only one pair this spring. The meadow larks are on duty in large numbers. They come into the trees of my yard and wind out their long, plaintive notes almost every day. This bird is an active, interesting fellow. His favorite position is the top of some tall tree standing out alone in the field. Frequently, as he runs before me in the grass, I discover a likeness to the quail. His nest is hardly more than a slight hollow in the ground, made habitable by a meager lining of grass and leaves. Their flight is heavy, though sometimes swift, and as they flutter down to the ground one is reminded of the bobolink. The male and female are quite similar in appearance, being mottled with brown and fawn color upon the head, back and wings, while the chin and breast are a bright yellow, the throat being crossed with a broad crescent shaped band of velvety black.

Of the woodpecker species, I have seen more of the yellow hammer than I have in many seasons before. This bird, though essentially of the woodpecker family, differs from them in finding part of its food on the ground. His list of local names is a long one. Besides the one named above he is called " flicker," " yucker," " highhole," " wood robin " and " yellow winged woodpecker." Years ago I found the nest of this bird only in the large forest trees. Latterly I notice he enjoys the fields more. In the long rows of maples on the Waterville road he is quite at home. He is not so particular as some of the other members of his family about boring into the decayed limbs of the trees for his nesting place. With his strong bill he easily shapes his house in the hard oak or maple limb, and once domiciled, is secure from most of his enemies. I know of no other bird that seems to enjoy the spring time with a richer relish than the yellow hammer. His peculiar but not unpleasant call rings out over the fields and through the woods like a bugle note. A part of his cheerier pastime is found far up on the great limbs of a tall tree, in what appears to be a genuine bird game of hide and seek. It is surprising with what celerity he will dart up and down and around the tree. He has the advantage of the squirrel in the aid of his strong wings and sharp claws which adapt themselves readily to every change of position.

One can easily determine the bird, not only by his call, but by his bright yellow color, also by the wavy motion of flight, and the large white spot displayed conspicuously on his back as he passes rapidly through the air.

Another member of the woodpecker family—the red-headed variety—seems to be disappearing. Formerly they were quite plentiful, numerous specimens being seen each season. This bird is justly celebrated for its brilliant plumage. The head and upper part of the neck are of a deep crimson, set off below by pure white, and above by a glossy steel blue. His natural food is insects, but he dearly loves different kinds of fruit, and is not at all averse to a feast of tender green corn   In my boyhood the old farm had its row of cherry trees extending along the roadside well down to the great wood. Redhead levied tribute on the fruit, and almost all the first ripening were marketed by him. How easily and

gracefully he would curve his way from the great
maples, and what an insatiable appetite for the lus-
cious red cherries he brought with him! A little
later we watched the members of the family as they
took their first lessons in flying. Many a tumble and
curve not laid down in the experience of the older
birds marked the first efforts of the young learners.
Very soon, however, they were adepts in the science,
and, we noticed, were almost certain to make the first
long flight to the old farm cherry trees.

Of the smaller varieties of this species we have the
yellow breasted woodpecker and the downy woodpecker, or sap-sucker, as he is sometimes called.
The yellow breasted is the larger, and like the redhead. seems to be disappearing in this section.
Downy, while not as active as the larger kinds, is a
favorite with most bird lovers. He rarely indulges in
a long flight, and apparently takes little or no notice
of visitors. It is an interesting scene in forest life to
note the work done by this little fellow in the passing
hour. A whirr of wings and he flashes by from some high
point that he has reached on a neighboring tree, and
alighting near the foot of a tall trunk, begins his
search for the eggs and insects hidden there. Round
and round he goes, looking into every cranny and
crevice, working slowly up towards the top of the
tree. Sometimes he hangs head downward under a

limb and ever and anon utters his peculiar note, which among all that I hear from the birds seems the richest in real contentment. I have known one a full hour in feeding over the pasture of a large tree. Sap-sucker, in his quiet way and cherry, patient note. is the bird of the forest. Dressed in his suit of gray, he harmonizes well with the color of the great tree trunks, and some way the single note of his homely song sounds like the breathing of the trees when the wind is playing through them on a quiet summer day. The larger member of the woodpecker family is found in the south and west. He is known as the ivory-bill and is truly a noble bird. His favorite resort is the tall pines and cypress of the vast swamps of the southwest. Wilson says : " Wherever he frequents he leaves numerous monuments of his industry behind him. We there see enormous pine trees with cart loads of bark lying around their roots, and chips of the trunk itself, in such quantities as to suggest the idea that half a dozen ax men had been at work there for the whole morning." I have seen the bird in his native haunts. and remarked the power with which he did his work. I never saw the nest, but am told that it is usually in a large cypress or cottonwood tree. The plumage of this bird is mostly black, with slight shadings of blue. The head is surmounted by a crest of long flowing plumes, those falling over the forehead of a jetty black, while those of the hinder part are a brilliant crimson. The Indians made use of the brighter feathers for some of their decorations, and the smooth ivory-bill enters into the mysteries of the medicine man's incantations. Like his northern brethren, ivory-bill has no gleam of the instinct of migration in his nature. With the entire family food is plentiful, winter and summer alike, so they simply eat, drink and are merry, after the fashion of birds, which, like the " laws of the Medes and Persians," is a fashion that alters not as the years come and go.

V.

Occasionally we have the beautiful sight of a large number of hawks sailing high in the air, apparently taking a spring pastime. This morning while at work in my garden, I heard the peculiar cry of the hen-hawk repeated many times. It came down from far above me, and I soon located the place. Directly over my head, perhaps a mile high, several great birds were circling slowly through the air in broad sweeps, moving from right to left, steadily passing toward the west. It certainly was the morning play of the birds, and never, at any other time of the day quite so striking and beautiful. The sun had not yet risen to me, but from the hawks, as they turned gracefully and without apparent motion of the wings, there was the flash of gold as from the surface of a great shield. I watched them several minutes before the sun was lifted into sight from where I stood. I never watch this movement of our great soaring birds without seeing new wonders in it. It is only the largest of our birds that can indulge in the recreation. Their large. but won-

derfully muscular and strong bodies are given the
expanse of wing that when spread in the upper air
seems to support the bird without any apparent effort on his part. I have watched closely with a
glass for many minutes at a time, and never detected
the least sign of a vertical movement of the wings.
The flight of the birds—of any of them—is always a
profound mystery to me, but this soaring of the
hawks is mystery of mystery. Some think that at
that high elevation there is a strong wind blowing
steadily so that the bird has only to set in position
and keep there the broad expanse of wing, and sail
the ocean of air as the ship sails the ocean of water.

I have a fancy that this only half reveals the secret of the art, but the hidden portion I can not
uncover. In fact, I enjoy the scene of the flight all
the more for having the details largely veiled. But
be that as it may, the soaring of the great birds far
up in the blue dome is a vision of beauty. Each
describes the arc of his own circle, but to the be-
holder they seem to intersect and cross each other
in bewildering succession. Very likely the birds
are quite a distance apart, though to one standing
below them, they appear to be on the same plane.
Now and then the coterie I was watching would
indulge in a series of aerial evolutions that would
throw all the ordinary movements to the winds. By

just a single motion, the bird would leave the circling sweep, and dart, with incredible celerity, down
through the great blue fields of air, until it seemed
impossible for any ordinary strength to stay the
flight.   A slight movement of wing or body, however,
would change the direction into a broad curve upward until nearly all the original height would be
gained, which a few strokes of the great wings would
complete, and the bird take his place with his fellows, cleaving the air quietly again as though nothing unusual had happened.   Sometimes two or more
of the hawks would make these side movements together.   Then the play would wax furious, and only
the largest space would suffice for such marvelous
sweeps of the great birds.   For an hour or more
they sailed and gamboled in my sight, then slowly
faded from view far over toward College Hill.   I am
told that there are days in the fall of the year when
the hawks assemble in such numbers that they are
termed " hawk days."   It is a new feature in the
country side which I have not personally observed.

The hawk is the freebooter of the birds.   Like Ishmael among his fellows, his hand is against every
man and every man's hand against him.   There are
many varieties of this bird ranging in size from the
little sparrow-hawk to the large hen-hawk.   Of the
larger size I do not observe as many as formerly.

though the smaller seem as numerous as ever. In the southwest, on the plains, I noticed several varieties not known in the east. One with the plumage nearly white was a handsome bird of the size of our large pigeon-hawk. The family on the great prairies conform nicely to the conditions, tucking their nests away in the crevices of the sides of the great canons which everywhere seam those vast plains. The nests of our species are placed in trees, and appear at a little distance like large bunches of fine sticks thrown together without much regard for order. Of necessity, there can be but little neatness in such a house, fed as the young are, with all kinds of small birds and animals.

The most active of the family that harbors with us is the pigeon-hawk. He bears several names, perhaps a confounding of varieties in the catalogue, such as American-hawk, sharp-skinned hawk, long-tailed hawk and others. He is easily distinguished, however, by his rapid flight, and by the unusual length of the tail. The movement of this bird on the wing is like the rapid flight of the arrow. I have seen him secure birds of most of the smaller species in fair open flight. Frequently I have known him to pay a visit to the old farm, coming into the yard with the rush peculiar to his movements. Instantly all was commotion. The barnyard fowls betook themselves to the sheds and secure places, but the poor doves fared harder. Sometimes before they could hide safely or secure protection in flight, one would fall into the talons of the bold depredator. It is not often, however, that the hawk will take the great risk of an attack on the farmyard. His hunting grounds usually are in safer places. It is a lesson in cunning and skill which the bird illustrates as he hunts in the open field. I have seen him hanging over a meadow searching with keen eye every inch of the grassy surface. Suddenly he would drop as the stone falls, and, striking the ground with a sharp thud, would arise almost instantly with some luckless mouse securely trapped in his strong talons.

There is in country places much prejudice still existing against the entire family of hawks. Doubtless it is quite natural, as the birds of this species do feast now and then on the best chickens the farmer can furnish, and otherwise present traits of character which are not pleasant to contemplate, still they fill a place in the economy of Mother Nature's large household, which is of vast benefit to the tiller of the soil. A very large portion of the food of the hawk consists of vermin of all kinds, so that it may be truly said of him that he is an important scavenger of the fields which can not be spared. We can well afford to spread his table occasionally with choicer viands than he is accustomed to have. Perhaps we can term such treatment a just return for many services which he unconsciously renders to the lords of creation ; and would it not be a nice influence to throw around our boys, teaching them the blessed reciprocity of good for good, even to the action which seems a return of good for that which lifts its head and looks like evil ?

VI.

Bobolink saluted us first on the morning of the 4th of May. The old rule of the country-side, " that bobolink appears with the first dandelion " has proven faulty this year. The dandelion had been in blossom more than a week when the bird gave notice that he was on summer duty again. I had been on the watch for him each morning, and more than once fancied the rollicking notes of his song were tumbling all around me. Watching for the singer, however, did not empty the coming entirely of the element of surprise, nor detract in the slightest degree from the ripple and rush of this " anthem of the meadows." Formerly, as now, this bird seemed to study the effect of his advent. Working in my garden, with many a moment given to watching that splendid vision of " the new heavens and new earth," bobolink comes like a spirit of the morning and my first salutation is the glad song poured down upon me from the leafy coverts of the nearest tree top.

This year and last he found his place in the waving branches of a tall birch and the first note of his

song—that liquid, smooth flowing note—stopped all
work and there was no renewal of the toil until the
singer had responded to at least three encores. Each
species of our spring and summer birds seems to
represent some part or phase of nature. The bobolink belongs to the meadows. His song is spangled
like the meadows. It ripples and waves and tumbles
as the grass does in the summer breeze. And the
bird seems to have gotten all this imbedded in his
very flight. Song and flight appear to be of one
mind and heart. Most of our birds sing when
perched in some fine place, and have hardly more
than a single note to dispense when on the wing,
but bobolink is the same free, joyous singer whether
sitting or flying. I am utterly at a loss to know how
the rush of merry notes finds place in that trim little
black throat. I have known many attempts made to
put the song in the black and white of the musical
scale, but I have never heard voice or instrument
that could render it as the bird does. It is a melody
of most pleasing sounds which simply defies descrip-
tion. To me it is the heart of the meadows enriched
with sunshine and balmy air—the lush grass and per-
fume of flowers, the dews and rains and the very
essence of the melody of the other field birds.

Bobolink has made some progress in civilization.
He has his Florida where he spends his winters, and

4

the gentlemen of the tribe change the color if not
the fashion of their dress twice during the year. For
at least six weeks after the spring arrival the male
bird pours out his unrivaled notes, then suddenly
drops his hilarity and becomes the soberest of housekeepers. When caring for the young the parent
birds utter almost precisely the same note, and so far
as I have observed, share equally in the home duties.
About the last of August the old and young birds
gather in great flocks—all now of the same color—
and after a few days of merry sporting in the hedge-
rows and fields, take up their journey toward the
winter home. It is largely a mystery this journeying.
When it begins, by what route it is prosecuted, whether
by long or by short stages, who knows? I have a notion
that a portion of the flight is so high in the air that the
naked eye can not reach the travelers, and also that
the clear moonlight nights are pressed into service
in forwarding the journey, but whether by night or
by day, by easy or by long stages, they come in large
numbers to the first stopping place among the great
reed marshes of Pennsylvania.

Here they frolic and feast until they attain to
double the size of the bird we know in the northern
meadows. Thousands are trapped and shot, and the
flesh is considered the great delicacy of the season.
From here they complete the journey, and we find

them a little later snugly domiciled in the rice fields
of the far south. No one would imagine that our
singer was hidden under the brown coat of one of
these rice gormandizers, but there he is and except
the common chirp of his species, makes no sound.
All winter long he feasts and plays right in the very
heart of the sunny south, and never opens his mouth
to utter the semblance of one of his bubbling notes.
Just why a new coat should loosen his tongue in song
I can not tell—in fact I do not believe it does. What
an old farmer friend of mine—dead and gone now
—called the "glorious bursting forth of our spring-
time" seems to set the songs free. Then of course
there is mixed with this the influence of that nuptial
chant which is the " light on our land and sea " in
the glad springtime.

Bobolink has a heart, and he uses it, too, and
when he falls to loving he falls to singing, like many
a swain of other name and nature. But even with
all the influences counted that we can reach, I
can not understand why for ten or eleven months of
the year he should be silent, only trilling his glad
song a meager six weeks out of the fifty-two. His
favorite resort is some meadow hillside sloping to
the east, flanked by an old apple orchard. A bough
of the apple tree, or some large stone out in the
field, is the resting spot from which he tells of the

joy that thrills him.   The nest, like that of the other
ground birds, is securely lodged in some slight cavity
of the meadow surface.   He shows some skill and
taste in construction, though these are evidently sec-
ondary in bobolink's idea of architecture.

The young don the sober winter attire of the
parent birds, and make no change until the following spring brings them to their northern homes.
Years ago an uncle of mine, of scientific turn of mind,
conceived the idea that the bobolink not only
changed the color of his plumage, but also the fibre
of his character.   His theory was that our snow
buntings were bobolinks masquerading under their
white waistcoats during the winter months, easily
turning back to the old brown and black when the
springtime came.   He captured some of the buntings and kept them through the year, and while his
knowledge was increased by his experience, one of
his pet theories was entirely dissipated.   Irving, in
his celebrated article telling bobolink's qualities,
good and bad, writes that in his freedom and gladness of song, he was the envy of every school boy
for miles around.   Surely our author might have
written that the merry singer moved to envy a much
wider field of hearts.   Certainly admiration and delight follow him, wherever he goes, when he is really
at his best.

His welcome has not even a gleam of anything narrow and selfish in it. He sings all there is of him into his song. He makes it a voice cheerily interpreting the great meadow nature of our hills and vales. He makes it all laugh and sing, and we laugh and sing with him.

VII.

The different species of summer birds, with the exception of one or two kinds are all present in their northern haunts, (May 18th). The cuckoo and the waxwing, and possibly some of the wood birds, have not yet arrived. The swallow family is in its place, and active, as it always is. We have three species of the true swallows,—the barn, cliff and eave swallows. The bird usually termed the chimney swallow does not belong to the swallow family, but is closely allied to the swift or night-hawk species. Songless as this large family is, still they are by no means unattractive. They are given the almost faultless grace of flight. Their place of beauty is on the wing, and it is only at rare intervals that they are found at rest during the day time. The barn swallow fastens his nest in some convenient place high up among the rafters of the old barn. He skillfully commands the mud of the roadway, dried grass, and the tiny feathers of the farm yard, and with many a deft swallow touch, shapes them all into a bird-house of no little strength and beauty. The old time

barns were made with the swallow hole cut in the end
high up near the point of the roof. In and out of
these openings the birds would dart the livelong day,
and not seldom would the boy, hot and dusty, tramp-
ing hay in the great mows, envy the swallow's glad,
free life. The song of this bird is hardly more than
a gentle twitter, uttered usually, when sitting at rest.
Most of the swallow's flight is sobered with work,
though now and then I think it is lifted into pastime. Anyone who has seen a little company of
these birds on a bright summer evening taking their
daily bath, will understand what I mean. Just at
the corner of the wood which covers Smith Hill all
down its southern slope, is cradled a little pond.
One of the delights of my boyhood was the swim-
ming parties which gathered here on the warm summer evenings. Often I would precede the boys an
hour or more, and from a cozy nook of the wood
side, watch the swallows as they came in troops of
a dozen or more to their daily ablutions. With
what grace they would curve down from the hills
on either side, and sweep along the surface of the
water! Now and then the wings would dip like oars,
and anon the body would drop below the surface for
an instant, and then emerge, scattering the water in
pearly drops far and wide. Over and over the bath
would be repeated, and the birds would hie away to

the great barn, their little bodies glistening like blades of grass polished with the morning dew.

The eave swallow differs from the barn swallow in many ways. They are easily distinguished by the whiter breasts and by the shorter and squarer tail. Years ago this branch of the family was largely represented here. Some of the large barns were thronged by hundreds of the birds. At Harvey Head's they found a nesting place to their liking. All along under the eaves of the barn, the nests were crowded like so many ant hills, thrust into place with an opening left just at the top. When the nests were building the birds came and went in a stream that flowed without ceasing all day long. The craft of the mason was called into vogue, and the house firmly, if not handsomely built. When completed, and the mothers' " at home " fully established, it was quite a social scene. The callers, I expect, were the happy husbands of the many wives, and though the coming and going were unbroken all the day, there seemed to be no confusion or lack of bird courtesy anywhere. It was a happy family, and the farmer above named found happiness in the birds' happiness. He provided a shelf nicely adapted to the birds' wants, and they repaid him a hundred fold in clearing the farm of troublesome insects. I am told that these swallows have disappeared from their former haunts, and one asks the question, "Where have they gone?" The farmer ought to ask it and press it to an answer pretty strongly. If the why of absence can be reached and removed, it surely ought to be done. My own opinion is that it is one of those movements of birds brought about by a variety of causes, for some of which man is to blame, that will be removed eventually, and the birds find their way to the old homes again.

The cliff swallow seems to differ but little from the eave swallow. Naturalists, I believe, class them as one family; still it seems to me there is a distinction. The nests of the cliff swallow are formed in a cliff or bank of sand. A hole is bored horizontally for several inches, then widened to sufficient size for the nest. It forms a very safe retreat from the birds' many enemies, though the wash of the bank sometimes brings destruction upon the entire village.

The chimney swallow, or swift, more correctly named, is a bird that ought to be familiar to all. It is almost the single bird family that comes into our houses to make its home. The chimney is its favorite nesting place, though the old hollow tree, open at the top, will serve its purpose. Its nest is a rude structure fastened to the side of the chimney by some glutinous substance which the bird manufactures for

the purpose. The architecture of the nest can well
be rude, as it is built where it is seldom seen, though
why it should not be stronger is a problem that my
boyish thought frequently sought to solve. Every
year the nests of the swallows were hung in the
chimney of the old farm house, and almost every year
some of them would come down with all the precious
freight of young birds nearly grown. The subdued
twitter behind the old kitchen fireboard would be our
first notice of the disaster. Removing the board
would show us the young family winking and blinking
in the soot and ashes, and vainly endeavoring to
clamber up the smooth back of the fireplace. A little help from the children would tide over the diffi-
culties of starting, and we would soon have the satis-
faction of seeing them far up the chimney side,
where they would meet the old birds and set up for
the remaining chimney days a rude sort of houseless
housekeeping that finally brought them all to the free,
glad life of the upper air. This bird has no equal in
the realm of flight. For swiftness, grace and beauty
it is all unrivaled. How it can pass and repass, de-
scribe its broad curves, rise far away into the open
blue, or drop and skim along the meadow surface all
day long on its rapid flight, how this can be with that
little body and wings, is to me the profoundest of
mysteries. Without any question his daily flight is

hundreds of miles, and when he takes his last evening
pastime before descending into the old chimney he
seems in freshness " to bring back immaculate the
manners of the morn." Sometime in the last of August
the swallows leave us and betake themselves to the
far away tropics for their winter outing. No doubt
storms and other vicissitudes greatly deplete their
numbers, but each spring enough find their way back
to gladden our summer time with the wondrous
grace and beauty of their marvelous flight.

VIII.

Our wood birds are now well domiciled in their northern haunts, (May 28). They evidence excellent judgment in selecting their summer homes. The hill, sloping nicely to the east, is their favorite resort. I have a half notion that they not only like the warmer eastern exposure, but have some taste in selecting the broad, open outlook. All along the range of our " Paris Berkshire," where it dips toward the beautiful Sauquoit valley, the wood birds find their ideal home. The old Butler farm two miles east of Sauquoit village, seems to furnish all the conditions of a bird paradise. Sixty acres and more of the western portion of the farm were cleared a few years ago. Part of this tract was allowed to grow up again with a rich variety of forest trees, and part was gradually brought into use as a large side hill pasture. The pasture is dotted here and there with clumps of young trees reaching back to the wooded tract, the whole forming a broad surface about equally divided between the higher shelf or plateau, and the slope reaching down to the valley below. The view from any part of this section is extremely fine, embracing the wide expanse of the Sauquoit valley, from the gateway near New Hartford, far up to the bend of the hills, where the creek comes tumbling down from the Summit Springs The writer asks his readers to take a stroll with him through this great park and note some of its feathered denizens which flash and love and sing in its truly beautiful bowers. My favorite approach is along the high ground on the back part of the old Wicks farm. From thence is a sharp descent of a hundred feet and more, to the western gate of the large grove. At my last visit the saluta-tion at the gate was that gem of bird melody, the song of the thrush. It came in that peculiar, fasci-nating trill that once heard is never forgotten, and as surely can not be described. In it is the heart of the sylvan aisles, all shaped and toned as one would wish the wood to sing to him. Again and again the song was repeated, all of it hushed, how-ever, as I climbed down from the old fence and threaded my way slowly among the trees.

What a sly fellow the thrush is! I just caught sight of this one's slender form as he rapidly slid away into the deeper recesses of the wood. A little later I shall find him with his mate, well set up in housekeeping, and, of course, not quite so shy. Here at the edge of the pasture I catch the song of

5

a bird which savors not a little of the open fields.
The little tree in the open glade is the stage from
which the singer pours forth his rich melody.
Perched on the very top of the tree, he sings away
into the blue air above him as though his very life
depended on the song being done quickly, and well
done too.   It is the little bluefinch or sparrow—
sometimes called the indigo bird.   The plumage is
a rich indigo blue throughout, and, like the song,
flashes in the sunlight as though it came out of the
deep blue of the far away sky.   The nest, no doubt,
was somewhere near, but I was too busy watching
the many wood dwellers to look it up then   As I
came down to the rude fence near the old wood
road, a bird glided by me that I quickly recognized
as the rose-breasted grosbeak.   A little rain was
falling, but with some indication of breaking away,
and I knew that the advent of the sun again would
loosen all the birds' tongues in song.   The flash of
the sunlight was the signal, and the song I was waiting for came almost instantly, with a dozen others.

I moved down to the edge of the pasture and
there in the full light of the sun the bird sat, pouring
forth a song that was rich with the witchery of bird
music. On the white breast flashed the spot of crimson which gives the bird its name, and it almost
seemed as though its fellows did reverence to the

singer, both on account of its beauty and its song. It is only occasionally that I discover this bird, and the day that reveals him is one marked with red letters in my calendar. A little farther on down on the border of the great ravine which seams the pasture and grove deeply on the northern side, I saw a bright flash of red among the great trees that here have not been cut away. It was that beauty of our forest glades, the scarlet tannager. Formerly the tannager was common to all our groves; now I find him but rarely. I think myself fortunate if I discover a single specimen during the season. With his wings and tail of jetty black, and body clothed in the most brilliant and glowing scarlet, the tannager stands all unrivaled for beauty of plumage among our many birds. He builds a shapely nest, but of such slight materials that the light may easily be seen through it. One would hardly imagine the female in her sober coat of pale green to belong to the same family. What she lacks in beauty, however, is made up in affection for her young. Hardly any other of our forest birds equal the tannager in care for the nestlings. Several of our naturalists speak of this characteristic as remarkable.

While watching the tannager I heard at the edge of the clearing the peculiar chirp of a bird that seems the busy fellow of all the wood songsters. I walked

quietly to a point near some low bushes and soon
discovered the object of my search, the little American redstart.   Among the large family of wood-
warblers, I should place the redstart first in point of
activity and not excelled in beauty of plumage.   I
find them altogether too busy to pay much attention
to me, so in watching them I can often draw so near
as almost to touch them.   I discovered this pair had
their nest in a low bushy tree, evidently just the beginning of housekeeping. · The male bird had but
few home duties to look after, so he showed me how
the redstart works and plays.   He would push his
way up among the thick branches, searching almost
every twig and leaf for insects, until at some favorable opening he would turn a somersault into the
air, which I thought was play, until I heard the little
bill snap and discovered that the side excursion was
a business foray into the midst of a bevy of flies.
The very work of such a bird is done with a zest that
seems to be nothing but play.

The trophies of the chase in redstart's realm must
be many hundreds every day.   The beauty of this
bird's markings distinguishes him in the warbler
family—the deep black which is the predominating
color, contrasting finely with the streaks and bands
of orange and vermillion on the sides, wings, and tail.
Going down into the deep ravine I picked my way

carefuly along the picturesque bank of a little brook
that tumbles down from the pasture above. Here
was less of bird life, but a lavish profusion of plants
and flowers. I saw signs that the raccoon was at
home in this secluded spot, and under the roots of
an upturned tree was the well chosen home of the
red fox. Long ago the fish disappeared from the
brook, and some of the larger trees lie moldering in
the damp, almost sunless, retreats of the steep hillside. But someway there was a luxury of enjoyment, lying on the mossy bank of the murmuring
stream, and looking away through the green leafy
avenues up to the broad ocean of blue that seemed
so far off from the bottom of the ravine. Some chimney swallows and two or three crows passed leisurely
over the roadway of the upper air, but seemed almost
wierd-like in the blue haze of distance. Why not a
little touch of " Distance lends enchantment to the
view ?"

IX.

June 1st, sitting on my porch just as the sun was
sinking low in the western sky, the evening song of a
great variety of birds was borne to my ear. It came from
all sides, and I was curious to know how many species
of the feathered songsters were represented in the
large choir. In the yard near by I readily detected
the following varieties : Robin, bluebird, grackle,
kingbird, large and small flycatcher, wren, yellow
warbler, vireo, small tree sparrow, vesper sparrow,
purple crown sparrow, yellow bird, bobolink, lark,
cuckoo, oriole, chimney and barn swallow, and farther
away, from the swamp side, came the harsh notes of
the jay and crow—more than twenty varieties in all.
It was just the hour when the farmer, wearied with
the heat and burden of the long day, was taking the
comfort of the easy chair. What music, I thought,
is given to rest and cheer in this concert of the birds.
The ear may not be trained to catch the secret of its
power, and it may be there is no conscious recogni-
tion of the influence, but there it is, filling the evening
quiet with what seems like the soft low notes of the

parting day. Every soul is better for the song, and all nature, animate and inanimate, is enriched by it. As the song was dying away with the coming of the darkness, the lawn directly at my door was the scene of one of those bird contests that, I suppose. occur much oftener than we know.

Just at the cemetery gate, a few hundred yards below the rectory, in a dense evergreen, is the nesting place of a pair of blackbirds. They set up first as housekeepers on the rectory lawn, and the very beginning of their enterprise was the signal for war. A pair of enterprising robins had preëmpted a claim in that spot, and near by, on the church lot, another family of robins was snugly domiciled, while a little farther down near the school house, still another pair had their home. I think blackbird could have made fair headway against a single pair of his enemies, but when they joined forces and brought in the yeoman of three distinct settlements there was nothing left for him to do only to abandon his half built house and take up a new claim. This he did with much protesting, and many a return for a short, free, spirited battle. I noticed in their battles that the forte of each party was the surprise. Blackbird would steal quietly along the line of trees at the roadside, and if he found robin napping, which was rarely the case, would fly full tilt against him, strike him sharply with his long dirk-like bill, then hie away with many a chuckle.   This game was played until robin adopted the plan of summoning his neighbors with a· few quick, sharp notes, and the whole trio of families would cross the border and fairly hunt their enemy down.   Victories among the birds are " on the side of the heaviest cannon." I noticed that the feud between these families grew as the young birds got large enough to need constant care.   Some way, then, all the " Old Adam " in the parent birds waked up and waxed hot and furious.   The blackbird got his nestlings ready for fight a little sooner than the robin.   Like all young birds just out of the nest, they went blundering around from place to place until finally, after an unusually long flight, one of the young grackle dropped upon my lawn hardly ten feet from the door.   One of the old birds came with it, and the advent of these two innocent looking bipeds was the signal for a conflict, or, rather, succession of conflicts, that lasted until darkness dropped its curtain and shut the eyes of the warriors.

The two robins tenting just at the house corner, began the fray.   They gave their peculiar war cry, and followed it with front, side, and rear attacks that were fairly bewildering.   It looked like a miniature case of the " Balaklava cannon," in the celebrated ride of the six hundred.   But the strategy of

Captain Blackbird was without a flaw. He piloted his little dusky charge across the lawn with marvelous skill, and before he was aware of it, found himself in the domain of the church robins. Like a fresh relay, they took the place of the first pair, and in much the same manner, escorted the intruders to the door of the school house yard. There the pair that were "lord of all they surveyed" from the low cornice of the old school house, came quickly into the contest. Their drum-beat was like the others, and the blows they struck much the same. Steadily, however, blackbird held on his way, and as the night fell, came out of the trying ordeal safe and sound, and I said: "Why not this a genuine 'Anabasis.' Xenophon and his ten thousand getting surely on and out of the enemy's country." The next morning the village school mistress discovered the "rank and file" of this masterly retreat snugly ensconced in the deep grass at the roadside, none the worse, apparently, for the trying experience of the evening before. In one form or another this battle will be repeated in birddom all the season through ; and the observer can not very well avoid propounding the query : "Why is this ? Why should these dwellers in our groves and fields live in a state of war ?" Surely there is room and food enough for them all. There is nothing to be gained by it that I can see,

only that it puts each bird on the keenest and most
vigorous kind of duty, and the conflicts call into
requisition every faculty of the warriors, and of
course, make the combatants stronger, if not better.
Among our song birds proper I have noticed that
the contest is usually between birds of nearly the
same size. The large and small do not quarrel very
much, except in cases where the birds of prey enter
into the contest. I surmise that the fiercer fights
like this between the blackbird and robin are incited
largely from the fact that one of the parties works
direct injury to the other, either upon the eggs or
the young. I have noticed the blackbird lurking
about robin's house, and I am pretty sure his errand
boded no good to the nestlings of redbreast's home.
My neighbor, who is a close observer, avers that he
has seen the marauder sucking and destroying the
eggs. He does not hesitate to speak some sharp
words through his breech loader, all of them in-
tended to make blackbird a better creature, as Sheri-
dan's Indians were transformed. I find myself,
however, loth to interfere in any of the battles which
the birds set in motion.

My hesitancy is partly due to the fact that I know
so little about the cause of the quarrel that it is not
at all easy to tell which party is really entitled to
my assistance, and partly to the other fact that my

best offices, when freely proffered, as a rule, only seem to make matters worse.

Just as I reached this point, an old army comrade dropped in to spend the day with me. His home is snugly tucked away at the foot of the Clayville hills, and he knows the birds and loves them. We found time to talk them over, sitting under the wide spreading apple tree of the open yard. The battle of blackbird and robin was the subject, when lo! the chuckle of the black fellow was just at our side. A moment later we discovered that his business was of a very practical character. In the evergreen near by, the foundation of his house was laid, and I suppose a few days more will see it completed. Clearly enough, the story I have been telling will be repeated ; that is, if robin sets up housekeeping near by, which he is very likely to do. If in the passage at arms there should be any new tactics worthy of record, I will try and save it in some future article of this chronicle of our feathered friends.

X.

Some years a single pair of orioles nest in the large trees near the rectory. This year three families of these birds are housekeeping within a radius of two or three hundred yards. In the early morning frequently the citizens of this realm hold a public meeting in my yard. I have no means of knowing just how they notify the different members of the council, but I have a notion that one or two of Master Oriole's clear notes would reach every member without much difficulty. At any rate the summons goes out and the birds hear and heed. It may be that questions of vast moment in birdland are discussed at these gatherings. I can not interpret the speeches word for word, but the spirit of the meeting speaks for itself. As the members all talk at once it is evidently a go-as-you-please convention. But, all levity aside, this morning talk of the orioles is one of the bright things in the rectory yard and is well worth a 4 o'clock waking to hear. The oriole is perhaps the most attractive in appearance of all our field and orchard birds. His suit of bright yel-

low, tastefully ornamented with glossy black, becomes his slender form well, and the rich notes of his
song, like one of the bird's names, are golden.

I know of no other bird of his size that excels him
in activity. The large apple tree in my yard is a
favorite hunting ground for oriole. I frequently take
a convenient seat and watch the operation. Perhaps the morning hunt has the most of the zest of
sport in it. The male bird is the sportsman—the
female I have never seen on duty in this way—and
the skill displayed is perfect after its kind. The
twigs and limbs are all traversed and re-traversed. If
a bug or a fly is overlooked it seems purely an accident. The fly-catchers proper will dart into the air
quite a distance in securing their prey, but oriole
reaches his with but very little use of the wings. The
movement by which he traps the fly seems very similar to the plan of the common garden toad. As I
see it, he appears to impale the insect with the sharp
point of the tongue. There is a quick motion of
the head and from the open bill a flash of bright
red, and the game disappears in the blaze as though
consumed on the instant. All my interviewing has
not yet quite determined just how it is done. A
little later in the season, however, I find this bird
busy in a work which has no hidden stroke. When
the tent caterpillar or apple tree worm has folded
6

himself away in his little cocoon house and doubtless feels perfectly safe, oriole improves the opportunity to make him useful in a manner not laid
down in the natural experience of caterpillars. I
have seen the search of the bird go on for hour
after hour all along the fence and underneath the
clapboards of the house and in the old abandoned
nests on the trees, so that each day he must destroy
a great number of the worms. I think from my observation that this forms the principal food of the
young of the oriole. One other bird—the little tree
sparrow—I notice, shares in this feast, and the two
together, I judge, are the principal means of keeping in check this pest of the apple tree.

The nest of the oriole is admirably constructed,
especially that of the species known as the Baltimore
oriole. I am told that in the south he hangs it on
the north side of the tree, but in the north it is usually swung from some pendent limb on the south side,
where for a part of the day at least the sun can fill it
with warmth and light. It is woven with rare skill,
all sorts of strings and bits of bark being used in the
construction. I have seen it suspended from the
long swinging branch of the elm or maple, the mother
bird sitting in perfect safety as the wind rocks and
sways her half-aerial cradle. Frequently this bird
will nest close to the house where busy men and

women go in and out day after day, and never dream that tenants at will are snugly fixed at their very doors. Sitting with a friend at the step of the house door, a slight sound called my attention to the swinging branch almost brushing the house directly over my head. A single glance revealed the pouch-like nest half concealed by a bunch of leaves that in a heavy wind would almost touch the house. The young apparently were half grown, and the happy householders were busy feeding four hungry fledglings that seemed never to have enough. I have a half notion that the nest of this bird, swaying in the slightest breeze, is a sort of preparatory school wherein the baby orioles are given some lessons in flight which forwards them wonderfully in that grace of motion.

The orchard oriole is the single other branch of this family that favors us with its visits. The name is derived from the fact that it generally nests in the apple orchard, and finds most of its food in that pasture. It differs from its Baltimore cousin in wearing a dress sobered almost to a reddish brown, and in the construction of its nest. The nest of this bird hangs like the vireos, from some convenient fork of the smaller limbs, and while it is strong and firmly built, it has but little of the tasty appearance of the other species. The orioles are not only general favorites on account of their brilliant plumage, but widely welcomed as singers of no mean order.   Oriole's song, however, is celebrated rather for the sweetness of the notes than for any particular prolonged melody, like the song sparrow or the bobolink.   As it comes to us first with the apple blossoms, it seems to interpret in some way the pink and white of these gems of the orchard.   The two or three notes slide into each other almost imperceptibly as the shades of color blend on the petals of the flowers, and though repeated many times during the day, never tire the listeners, in fact, are only restful as the senses find joy over and over in the beauty and fragrance of the orchard flowers.

A little episode of genuine bird scolding, closely associated with oriole, has been one of the daily scenes witnessed in my yard.   A little fly-catcher had brought his mate, and together they had put their cabin in a safe fork of the apple tree, and so far as I could see, were quite happy in their domestic bliss. I noticed nothing unusual in the bird life of the yard until the advent of the orioles.   The moment they appeared was the signal, not for war, for there was no fighting—but for an outburst from my family of flycatchers of the most vigorous kind of bird scolding· The noisy jargon was poured out with great vigor, and as oriole paid no attention to it, I concluded that

either he did not understand it, or it being entirely un-
called for on the part of the small neighbor, was best
mended by being unnoticed.

I have never seen the oriole in any way trench-
ing on the rights of his smaller neighbor, yet he
never appears in the rectory yard without fly-catcher
and his wee bit of a wife, filling the air with a storm
of the hottest kind of bird protests. Oriole, as I
have said, pays no attention to it, so I half surmise
that it is a sort of pastime for him, and perhaps flycatcher finds some fun in berating his big brother
where there is not the least bit of danger of any sharp
return stroke. Now and then, as in the above, I
find the birds human enough so that I make a note
of it, and wonder whether it is one of the many rifts
in the cloud which, for the time being, hides a fellowship that lies along the wide relation of all life.

THE HUMMING BIRD.

XI.

The largest family among the birds is the one of the smallest individual members. The humming bird is so small and of such delicate structure, that one hardly feels like classing it among the birds at all. The flight is almost literally a flash through the air. How that little body can be propelled at such marvelous speed is one of the profound problems of bird motion. The most rapid of our railroad trains can not equal this little creature as it darts away through the gardens and fields. The ordinary flight, I believe, is rated at nearly a hundred miles an hour. The strokes of the tiny wings defy all following with the eye, and the humming sound emitted gives the bird its name.

This bird's method of taking its food sets at defiance all rules of quiet, easy feasting. He takes all his meals on the wing. Just how he balances himself so nicely on those vibrating levers, and touches the right spot in the flower with his long slender bill, is a secret that I can not uncover. As I see it, however, it is done with dispatch and apparent ease.

Surely, it is the feast delicate among all the wide tables spread for our feathered friends. The wonder is how the little body holds so many sips. Two varieties visit and nest with us, though I think the little ruby-throat is gradually becoming our single representative of this great family. Naturalists tell us that this order of birds includes over 400 varieties. They are widely distributed, but essentially denizens of the tropics.

I am told that on some of the mountains in Central America, ten or twelve different kinds have been discovered, all of them nesting there, and making that one place their home. It is a curious fact that of this largest family of birds so few have been moved by the instinct of migration. Throughout the entire United States I believe only seven varieties have been found, and these only as summer visitors, even in the far sunny south.· Belonging, as this bird does, to the tropics, he puts on the brilliant attire that is characteristic of that favored region. Our own tiny visitor—the ruby-throat— though one of the least conspicuous of the entire family, has some touches of brilliant color. He seems to reflect the brightness of the flowers among which he passes most of his active life. I have noticed in my garden that ruby-throat comes in almost entirely by the same door. I hear the whirr of

wings, and I know just where to look for the visitor.
His flight is down from the old church, as though
right out of the morning sun just peeping over the
roof.   Very likely his nest is in the orchard on the
eastern side of the village, and he sets a good ex-
ample in this first movement of the day churchward.
At any rate that is the way he comes, and the going
is always a flash out over the old schoolhouse away
to the pine grove beyond.   Some writers tell us that
part of the food of the humming bird is the minute
insects that the bird readily sees and secures, though
they are almost too small for the human eye to detect.
I have never been sure, from my observation, that
this is true. I hear the snap of the tiny bill, but that
it means the trapping of the fly is not so certain.
Sipping the nectar of the flowers, why shouldn't the
happy fellow bring his bill together as the boy
smacks his lips over the sweets that relish with the
keenest delight ?   Some way it seems to me more in
keeping with this bird's size and character, that it
should live on the rich juices of the flowers.   A
blossom of the blossoms, part of the " house beautiful," so its every word out of the mouth of God, the
very fragrance of life.   Of all this great family it is
written " practically songless."   Occasionally one
hears from them a sound that is the faint imitation
of bird-song, just a thin, prolonged, single note.

The nest is a gem of bird architecture. I have
seen but one, and that long years ago.

My brother and I, taking the daily frolic in the
orchard on the old farm, came upon the little house,
hardly larger than an acorn cup. It was fastened to
the limb of the tree, and in color was so like the
limb that it was only by accident that we discovered
it. It was marked by great delicacy of structure, and
held two tiny white eggs not much larger than our
smallest peas. Curiosity satisfied, we left the pair
to the orchard quiet. A day or two later, however,
some enemy invaded ruby's home, and we lost our
opportunity for a more extended acquaintance with
this most interesting bird.

The humming bird is a great lover of freedom.
The wild, free life of the fields and gardens is the
home to his perfect liking. I do not know of a single
instance where he has lived more than a few
weeks in confinement. Occasionally it is well to put
the prison bars about some of our feathered friends.
Interesting facts are uncovered in this way, but at
best it does not give information of the richest character. The bird in confinement is only the shadow
of a bird. The limitations forced upon him chill his
spirit and cramp all his movements. Under such
conditions he can not be himself, for all is second-
hand. Some way his entire life is ever saying to

man, " Hands off if you would know me at my best."
To me no other kingdom of earth's many kingdoms
of life offers more of the gladness that is active, un-
trammeled, free ; but it must be in and out of its
own.   In brief, it must be on the wing—its "to and
fro," like the wind which bloweth where it listeth. To
know the bird is to know him at home, in the house
not built with hands, and who shall say that the far
off towers thereof are not lifted "eternal in the
heavens ?"

XII.

Perhaps among all our birds there is none less known than the owl. Spending his waking time while almost all other creatures sleep, he is not easily seen and studied. I fancy most of us think his life must be shaded even to a deep settled melancholy. Surely his work, and pastime, too, for that matter, are all done away from the light of day, but that his deeds are evil does not by any means follow. He has his place in the economy of nature, and fills it with the same fidelity that belongs to his fellows. Formerly, I think, these birds of the night were much more plentiful than now. It does not appear that their food has grown less, but rather that their homes have disappeared. Fifty years ago the great forest trees were standing, and his owlship had his choice of homes among many that were all desirable. Now the trees are gone, and with them the homes. A member of the owl family stands as a connecting link with the hawk family. It is known as the hawk-owl, and is found in the northern regions of both continents. It has the body and general form of the hawk, but the radiating feathers around the eyes and bill, as well as the form of the legs and feet, at once distinguish it as an owl.   It hunts its prey by day, and is noted for its boldness, sometimes taking the game from the hunter after it is shot.

While the greater number of the owls proper are nocturnal in their habits, there are two or three kinds that are active on the wing in broad daylight.   Of the smaller varieties of this class the burrowing owl of the plains is perhaps the best known.   They are found principally in the prairie dog towns of the west. They nest and breed in some abandoned burrow of the dogs, and seem to be on good terms with their neighbors.   I have seen them sitting like statues on the little mound of earth, at the house door.   Occasionally a dog would dart at them, sending them screaming into the air ; but in a few moments they would settle down again to the old musing attitude. I never saw them searching for food, but conclude that they found it in the almost innumerable insects that swarm in those treeless regions.   One day owl, notably conspicuous, is the great white or snowy owl of the Arctic regions.   Its· nesting place and home, largely, is far north in the Hudson Bay country.   Its plumage in the winter is of a beautiful snowy whiteness, sometimes marked, especially in the summer season, with spots of brown.   Frequently in the coldest winter weather these birds will wander down into the United States, extending their journeys sometimes as far south as Kentucky. Audubon gives an account of one which he saw near Louisville, Kentucky, engaged in the rather unusual occupation of catching fish. It is the only instance within my knowledge of anyone observing the owl thus occupied, and I find myself wondering whether the great naturalist was not nodding a little.

Thirty years ago the snowy owl was quite a common visitor in Central New York. Now it is seldom seen. In my boyhood days a family. residing on the hill south of the village, were aroused early on a cold morning in January, by an unusual noise behind the board which shut out the great fireplace in the old kitchen. The chimney flue. cautiously opened, revealed an arctic owl of the largest size. After a stout battle he was captured and consigned to a wooden cage. He proved a prize indeed, and seemed to enjoy confinement so long as his larder was well supplied. After a time. however. he ceased to be a novelty, and his captor, tiring of his company, opened the cage door and allowed him to depart upon his long flight northward. The other owls of this vicinity are the great-horned, the long-eared, the short-eared, and the little screech owl. The latter is the most abundant species, and there is

7

scarcely any section of the eastern or middle states where it is not found. Almost all are familiar with its melancholy notes. Most of our country boys, at one time or another, have been interviewed by this diminutive fellow. One half conjectures that a part of the wierd hooting is bird laughter following the flight of the thoroughly frightened boy. It does seem like the uncanny voice of the night, and I should doubt the saneness of the boy who was not alarmed by it. It is now many years since I have seen a specimen of the larger species. The last time I saw the great horned owl was back in the forties. My brother and I were dropping the plaster for the corn planting near the old swamp woods, at the southern gate of the farm All the morning, from where the hemlocks were thickest, there came a succession of sounds that told us of some sort of bird convention. At first it was almost exclusively the crows that did the talking. Gradually, however, this changed, and the bluejays took the floor. While they did not rival the crow in loudness, they excelled him in the sharp biting stroke. Finally, after an hour or more of the noise, we climbed over the old worm fence and worked our way carefully down to the swamp side. Without disturbing the disputants, we soon discovered the bone of contention and also just what the several parties had to

say about it. In the thick part of the old hemlock
sat a great horned owl. Evidently he had been be-
lated about his home getting the evening before, and
some sharp-eyed crow had discovered the poor wan-
derer and called his fellows to add a little more dis-
comfort to his helpless plight. They had their fun,
and then the jays came in for their share. I remember it was a most ludicrous scene. On every
side of the owl the jays were perched, and every one
of the dozen or more was ringing out his sharpest
cry. The object of all the outcry sat winking and
blinking in the light as though he was utterly bewil-
dered by the babel of sounds. On the part of the
jays the entire scene appeared to be a venture of
pure teasing. though had the owl been a smaller
bird, I doubt not he would have been much more
roughly used, for the jay, as some one has said, is
the "pirate among the birds."

The food of the owl consists very largely of the
smaller animals, especially of those that are nocturnal
in their habits. Sometimes the larger species visit
farmyards and levy tribute on the plump chickens
that roost in the old apple tree at the house door.
From the fact, however, that the large owls are rarely
found free from the strong odor of the skunk, we
know that this animal forms a large part of their food.
Night for their work, and pastime, with food odorous

as the above named, makes up a bird life that is almost entirely devoid of the glad things usually found in that kingdom.

XIII.

' There is one bird of size, color and emphatic voice that, like "the poor," we have with us always. Everybody knows the crow, and knows, too, that his place is a large one among our feathered friends. The simple fact that he continues with us is strong evidence of the "survival of the fittest." In all the early history of this section the crow was suffered simply as a nuisance. He had no rights that anyone in any way felt bound in the slightest degree to respect. The fiat went forth from every farmer and hunter, "death to the crow." It had the effect to render this black fellow the brightest, keenest, most wary of all our birds. Much has been written of his shrewdness, and more of his watchful skill whereby he outwits all his enemies, and still I fancy the half has not yet been told. In recent years a change has come over our rural districts, and our friend of the somber dress has profited by it. Men, especially farmers, have slowly learned that the crow is not an enemy, but a stout and most serviceable friend. He does some harm in the corn fields, and in other particulars is not altogether free from actions that complicate his character among our rural citizens, but on the other hand, he is of great service to the farmer. No other bird is so destructive to grubs and different kinds of the large insect pests as the crow.

Where the grasshoppers assemble he finds his richest pasture, and there is no limit to his appetite for snakes, toads and frogs. As by instinct, he discovers the animal that has fallen dead by the wayside. I have seen the crow almost instantly find its way to the single dead animal and in a brief space of time twenty of his fellows would be feasting with him. I could not discern any particular signal, and yet I suppose one was given, or the news transmitted in some other way. I have seen the same thing occur with the turkey buzzards of the Southwest. On the great open plains the body of a dead animal could be exposed but a few minutes before the buzzards would begin to assemble in large numbers. Not a bird in sight at first, then a single black speck in the far away blue, and then another, quickly growing into a long line of great birds all hastening to the feast. It may be an instinct that guides, or it may be the sharp sight of a watchful sentinel penetrating far beyond what we know of human vision. As a scavenger the crow is most useful. He has a fondness for the eggs and young of other birds, which he indulges with the utmost freedom. His size and strength enable him to attack and rob with impunity, though occasionally he meets with his match. The kingbird or giant flycatcher, does not hesitate to oppose him to the face, and is almost sure to dis·comfit him. I have seen the kingbird pursue the crow with such vigor as to alight on his back and apparently drive his sharp bill deep into the flesh of the bold marauder.

Some of the habits of the crow are quite peculiar. His shyness is proverbial, also his extreme watchfulness, but that this solemn fellow is possessed of what appears to be a keen sense of humor is not so generally known. They have, I think, their playgrounds where they take genuine crow pastime. I have noticed that the broad hillside just west of Cassville on the old Thomas farm, is one of their favorite resorts. In the hundreds of times that I have passed there I do not now recall a single occasion, either in winter or summer, when a larger or smaller flock of crows was not present, and almost always engaged in what looked like play. Of course, they know the best places for the pastime which suits their facetious moods, but inasmuch as they make such extensive use of the hillside, I think we may safely say their principal recreation is coasting. That certainly is what it looks like to me. The great black fellows

will come into sight, lumbering heavily along over
the crest of the hill, but the moment they drop into
the down grade, they glide easily to the hill foot,
where with a broad curve they sweep around by a
gentle ascent to the upland again.   They have the
advantage of the boys, for their hill, winter and summer alike, is always in order, and they seem to have
a little of the sport every day.   Some of their peculiarities are seen only where the young are taken
from the nest and thoroughly domesticated.   They
are easily tamed and for a time, at least, are interesting pets.

A friend favored us with a fine specimen last summer which rejoiced in the name of Croker.   He
quickly put away all the sly crow nature, and became as contented and familiar as the house cat.
His capacity for mischief seemed almost unlimited.
The old shingles on the barn he pulled out and scattered about the yard.   He sampled freely the first
ripe berries and apples.   He bored clean holes in the
squashes and pumpkins, and his particular delight
was to appropriate to himself all the brightest blossoms of the flower garden.   Frequently in the morning he would come into the garden where I was at
work, and after standing about for a while, first on
one foot and then on the other, eyeing curiously all
my motions, he would sidle along to some shrub, or

hill of corn, and after saluting it crow fashion, would circle about it, dancing and chuckling as I have seen the Indians do at some of their festivities. He seemed to enjoy the fun of a surprise. He would come slyly from a convenient perch and drop upon the shoulders of a person suddenly, and in proportion to the alarm his advent occasioned would be his apparent enjoyment of it all. On Sundays he made due effort to attend church ; in fact, he was so persistent that we were obliged to shut him up securely until the service was over. He resented these forced imprisonments, and never failed to express by his manner what he thought of such tyranny, as he walked slowly out of his cell. He seemed quite delighted when he learned his pranks were not appreciated, and we soon found that his most assiduous attentions were given where he appeared to know they were not wanted. He finally distributed his friendship so widely that he became a sort of village nuisance; and we felt obliged to return him to his farmhome. There he flourished for a time, but eventually indulged in so much mischief that he was turned over to the executioner, and so ignominiously ended his career.

As a nest builder the crow is not of high rank. In some convenient tree he piles together a mass of sticks, shaped for his purpose. The lining of the nest is hardly more than a thin veneering of finer sticks. The eggs are usually four in number, and the growing young are as noisy and hungry a set as can be found in the whole range of birddom. Formerly in the fall of the year this bird gathered in flocks of vast numbers. They scattered during the day time to feed, returning to the roosting place at night. I have seen them just before sundown pouring into the wood on the old Addington farm in a continuous stream until acres of trees were filled with them. For an hour or more there was a babel of sound that filled the entire country side, then with the subdued chuckle in which the crow indulges, they settled into a quiet, more or less fitful, until with the first ray of morning light they streamed out to the day's work and play. Later on the great flocks dissolved into companies of three or four, which were scattered far and wide for the somewhat meager feasting of the long winter. Perhaps the most picturesque appearance the crow makes is when he forms a feature in the winter landscape. He contrasts well with the whiteness of the snow, and some way the tones of his voice are always more or less chilly. If they smack at all of the poetic it is of the arctic kind, which has its place and power where the snow and cold reign supreme.

XIV.

The bird Ishmael. according to a more or less popular notion, is the English sparrow.   Like the colored brother from Africa, he landed on our shores without any choice of his own.   Once here, however, he proceeded to multiply in, if not to replenish the earth.   As long as he remained a "hewer of wood and drawer of water," he was thought nice, wise and useful.   He fell into line early as a new recruit, answered readily to roll call, and was regarded as steadily and surely moving on to all the immunities of American citizenship.   But like all the foreigners who had preceded him, once in possession of his footing on the new shore, he immediately asserted his rights and marshalled all his battalions to defend them.   He became a true American.   The spirit of freedom took possession of him.   If any ship sailed into his port ladened with the "tea of contraband," he tumbled it overboard without any particular ceremony, and I never heard that he put on another bird's warpaint in doing it.   If a sister commonwealth massed its troops, over came sparrow forces

and drove him out, it was done by hard fighting, and
so far as I have observed, there is enough human
nature in the English sparrow to impel him to battle
his way in again to the full possession of his own, if
the slightest chance occur favorable to his purpose.
I like this bird because there is so much real push
in him.   Transported to a distant land without his
consent being asked, he doesn't spend a moment's
time lamenting the matter.   He never whines nor
mopes.   He asks no favors of anybody.   He takes
matters just as he finds them.   He goes to work,
builds his house, marries, sets up housekeeping,
provides for his own, and keeps on, day after day,
enjoying that poor, weak, shaky song of his, just as
rapturously, for anything I can see, as Bobolink, the
Jenny Lind of our meadows, trills his matchless
melody.

How true it is that the core of the song lies a
great deal deeper than the execution which simply
awakens our admiration. The strong, true, right heart
never knows any discord, and I fancy our homely
sparrow must be the possessor of a pretty good heart,
or he never could get on so contentedly for even one
hour with that "breaking forth" of his to which it
hardly seems possible to apply the appellation of
" joyful noise." The virtue of contentment under
adverse circumstances surely is here.

Expatriation, voice and raiment never in the slightest degree artistic, never much more than "the against every man," but with this a certain kind of self-assertion that rises often to the dignity of real courage, and a sort of dogged persistence that, Grant-like, never knows defeat,—why is not this sparrow the typical Teuton of the bird races—the victory-winning fellow because he attends to the winning of the victory, and to that alone? But let us turn to what the sparrow is in real every day life as he passes in review under our own observation. Most of the birds give us a part of their lives only, but the sparrow the round year, with all his hopes and fears and loves. The merit of industry is surely his. He is a worker that needeth not to be ashamed. I have watched a pair at their nest building when it seemed a task without any release. No other bird of its size brings together such a quantity of material. He piles it up day after day, and, seemingly, when the nest is done he goes on piling it up. Almost any place that is large enough will do for sparrow's home. He will bear a good deal of adversity in the way of opposition to his house building. I have seen the nest removed when half built several times, and the bird keep right on rebuilding in the same place without any appearance of irritation. Sometimes the only way to stop the work is by clos-

8

ing up the place altogether. I think them true Ice-
landers in love of home. We have no other bird that
builds to stay like the English sparrow.

I conclude that the rising generation rarely ever
thinks of emigration as a relief to their over-crowded
towns—in fact, they have no over-crowded towns.
There is room and to spare on all their best streets,
and all are best. But industry and love of home shine
brightest where they have the golden setting of high
courage. Our bird, so far as I can learn, like Bis-
marck's Germans, "fears nothing but God." I do
not think he is as quarrelsome as some allege. I
have seen several contests that could be truly termed
civil war, but I have never seen very much fighting
between sparrow and our native birds. When he is
ranging a little beyond his own hearthstone most
birds have the ability and the disposition to drive
him back, but I have never known the battle joined
at his own door without sparrow standing strong for
all his rights. I like him because as a true English-
man he stands up for his rights.

In defense of his home he is quite ready to die
long before the enemy reaches the last ditch. That
such a spirit should at times develop many an Ishmael, I am quite prepared to believe, though it has
not been in my way to detect one. There is another
characteristic of this bird which is still a matter of

dispute.   His value as a worker in orchards and
gardens is widely questioned.   I have never seen
him aiding in any manner to enlarge the gardener's
hope, but in the trees I have noticed him on duty
many times.   Just what insect he eats I do not know ;
but through my glass I have watched the bird as he
moved along the upper side of a large limb, turning
over the loose pieces of bark and securing either
the insect or its eggs in large numbers.   I have never
discovered any harm to plant or shrub or tree
wrought by these little fellows.   One other trait of
character not often noted endears this bird to me—
a keen sense of humor.

A great commotion in the tree near my study
window one bright morning attracted my attention.
A dozen sparrows were tumbling about the branches,
shouting and chattering as though absorbed in some
kind of a bird game.   Suddenly they gathered in a
little knot in the thickest part of the tree and, peer-
ing in each other's faces, seemed to say, " What
next ? "   As though a signal had been given, the
bird on the highest twig reached down and, seizing
the one below by the feathers of the head, swung
him from the perch back and forth for nearly a
minute, then dropped him to a long tumble through
the branches as a boy would have bumped his way
along, until, clear of the tree, he caught the air with

his wings and flew merrily away. All this time the other birds stood on tiptoe with extended wings, keeping time apparently to the movement of the bird suspended in the air. If it were not an instance illustrating sparrow's love of a practical joke, then I do not know where to class it. Finally, this sparrow is the only one of our smaller village birds that habitually braves the rigor of our northern winters. He stays right on and for aught I can see, is the same contented fellow when the mercury is at zero as on the balmiest summer day. Why has he not really won his spurs in a most vigorous fashion here on our western shores? And why can not we, by a rule that we honor in every other direction, extend a cordial welcome to the bird that combines so many good qualities and possesses so little that we ever think is objectionable in the human brother?

XV.

In the deeper glades of the old cedar swamp we find some of the most interesting of our feathered friends. Perhaps the shyest of all our birds dwells here. He belongs to the large grouse family, and is easily a prince among his fellows. He is commonly designated by the name of partridge, which is oft-times somewhat confusing, as the common quail is also given the same local name. The range of this bird is of wide extent. He is equally at home in Southern New York and in the far northern region of the Hudson Bay country. To know him intimately requires no little skill and patience. One might pass a long lifetime in close proximity to partridge's home, and see but very little of him. The old farm where I spent all my early years was deeply fringed on its western border by a dense cedar swamp. It covered many acres of ground, and was the favorite resort of all the boys for miles around. In those leafy isles I first learned of the partridge and his many interesting habits of life. How he would flash out of the swamp sometimes, and come

swiftly to the old farm house, once dashing against
the roof and falling dead at the very dooostep.
Several times we found the bird sitting solemnly in
the old barn, apparently wondering as much as we
how he came there.

Again and again we tried the experiment of trans-
ferring the eggs to the brooding care of a motherly
hen, and always with the same result of the young
partridges scampering away into the grass the moment they were hatched. On his native heather,
however, the partridge is a proud and merry citizen.
I have watched him many times, and I know of no
bird that seems to make more of life. I recall a
little group that I came upon in an old lumber road
just at the swamp side. It was early morning
and the birds were evidently out for an hour or two
of merry-making. From the vantage ground of a
thicket of cedar I could see them clearly without
my presence being in the least suspected. They ran
rapidly down the road for a little distance, then with
a brisk flutter of the wings, retraced their steps. Curiously they would peer into the thickets on either
side, and at times almost seem to dance over the
mossy carpet, keeping step together. Suddenly one
of the birds scurried away to a large half buried log,
and I saw for the first, and only time in my life, that
peculiar action known as the " drumming of the

partridge." Standing high on his feet, the bird passed rapidly along the log, striking his wings together in front of the body, giving out a low muffled sound not unlike distant thunder.

Some one has called it the "song of the partridge." Evidently it has to do with the merry making of the bird, and possibly may be of more serious significance. As it occurs only in the spring of the year, I am quite sure there is a nuptial strain in it. But at this particular time it seemed to be pure fun making, at least so it appeared to me. At another time I was sitting quietly among the tamaracks, watching a pair of hawks at their nest building, when my attention was attracted by a slight rustle among the leaves. Glancing in the direction of the sound, I was given a fine view of a large partridge passing quietly on a tour of inspection. He had discovered me, and evidently was curious to know what sort of new being had dropped into the old swamp. Very slowly he passed me in review, describing nearly an entire circle in the effort; then, apparently quite satisfied, he walked deliberately away to his family, which I could hear at their morning duties a little further on among the trees. I am sure that if this shyest of birds was given immunity from the hunter, he would become much more familiar, and we should find him a most entertaining companion. The nest is usually snugly tucked away in some half concealed place, though I have discovered it in the open glade where there was little or no cover. The young birds seem to hatch, as it were, at the same time, and all leave the nest immediately. The little fellows are wonderfully strong and active. They grow rapidly and are soon able to use their wings and fly short distances.

One of the most interesting scenes in swamp life is a family of these birds busy with the cares and play of partridge life. If nothing disturbs the housekeeper during the nesting days the group of children is a large one, frequently numbering fifteen and even more. On one of my journeys of swamp inspection I came upon a large family of these birds, the young not large enough to fly. Instantly there was a great commotion. The old birds flew into my face and about my head, and when the young ones had hidden nicely the mother bird went fluttering along the ground in a lame shambling fashion, as though she had been badly hurt and was hardly able to make her escape. Knowing it to be a ruse, I followed a little distance, then returned to the place where the young birds were hidden. The thick carpet of leaves and moss made an ideal hiding place.

A spot ten feet square held the birds, but I could not see one of them. I set my dog to the task of finding the little fellows. He quickly located each one, and I soon had fifteen housed safely in the old straw hat that served for the coop admirably. I was strongly tempted to take them home with me, but the stirring appeals of the parent birds quickly settled the case. I turned the hat over, and like a flash the fifteen disappeared in the leaves and moss. Ten minutes later I saw from a distance the happy reunion of parents and children, and the trooping away into the deeper recesses of the swamp.

Partridge has many enemies. The sportsman seeks him as the prince of game birds. Skunks and some of the larger birds find the eggs to their liking, while the sly fox gathers many a bird into his somewhat meager larder. Wet, cool weather reduces the number of the young chicks rapidly, while a winter of deep snow and severe cold will starve many of the older birds. At his best, however, the partridge is essentially the bird of the swamp. His sober mottled attire harmonizes well with the shadowy glades he makes his home, while the song he beats out with his wings, muffled and solemn, seems to come from moss-covered depths that can only find voice in the deep under-tones of sound. That his flight should be quite so swift is a little out of keeping with his place, but it may be a partial compensation for a life that is passed almost wholly in the shadowy reaches of the swamp or the denser thickets of the upland.

XVI.

One of the merriest dwellers in the rectory yard is the wren. A pair of them moved in about the middle of May, and I have noticed that their active life has been very accurately bounded by their wakeful moments. Usually I can discover the nest without much difficulty, but this year I have not been keen enough to detect it. I rather enjoy being outwitted by a bird. There is a spice of comfort in it that does not appear when one is left a little in the rear by his fellow man. This pair of wrens have pastured very pleasantly in my domain, and I have interviewed them almost every day, but as yet have not crossed the threshhold of the house where they live.

But what matter really? The head of this small family has sung to me daily. With his busy helpmeet he has taught me many a lesson in the most cheery kind of work-life, and socially I have no fault to find with any of the bird's ways. Among all the great hosts of my tenants-at-will I rank the wren very high. What a bright-eyed, active, generous little fellow he is! With the same breath he sings and

works and plays. He never seems to be out of
work, and. I am sure, sings right out of the gladness
of his merry little heart. It is quite a problem with
me when I am watching the smaller birds how the
insects manage to continue in existence at all. My
pair of wrens must secure thousands every day, and
a dozen other kinds of birds rival them in their work.
But I have no great concern about the matter.
Mother Nature takes care of her own, and while she
has mouths to feed, she will see to it that ·· seed time
and harvest " alternate without any great irregular-
ity. If I were to find the nest I am pretty sure
there would be no new thing discovered. Out in the
old orchard back of the hotel I fancy the house is
built. Some one of the many crevices in the old trees
holds it securely, and such feasting as goes on there
is only rivaled by some other bird household. A few
days more and the wrens' housekeeping will be over
for this season. The family will separate, and for ten
months or more will roam wild and free. But when
another spring-time comes, some part of the family
will come again to the old hearthstone, and so the
simple housekeeping may be repeated, perhaps for
generations.

There are three species of wrens that come to us.
The house-wren that we are all familiar with,
the great Carolina wren that frequents the water

courses, and the winter wren. which makes its visits
in the winter.   I am told that west of the Mississippi
there are several kinds that differ in some particulars
from our eastern species. but wherever they are
there the best of bird domestic life is found.   The
song of the wren is easily recognized, and I know of
no other bird that puts more of the home strain into
its melody.   I have fancied at times that its cheery
movement was the best expression of the fireside life
that we have among the birds.   It is closely akin to
the "cricket on the hearth " music, and finds its way
surely to the heart that is open to the sacred influence of home.   Another of the dwellers in the rectory
yard is in some respects an ideal bird.   He comes
early and sings with a sweetness all his own.   This
year I was sitting under the spreading branches of
my one large apple tree. about the middle of May,
when a familiar chirp attracted my attention.   Not
ten feet from me, hanging head downward and peer-
ing into my face curiously, was my bird, just arrived
from the sunny skies of the far south.   I had no
means of determining whether he belonged to the
family which stopped with me last year.   He certainly appeared perfectly at home, and was dressed
precisely as the man of the house was last season.
Through an opening in the leafy screen above, the
sun flashed down upon him, and when the reflection

reached me it brought the purple hue that told the
name of the bird, the "purple crowned sparrow."
Of course I answered his greeting, and assured him
the freedom of the rectory city. With some bipeds
I have now and then had such a burst of confidence
betrayed, but with the birds, never. They know how
to be perfectly at home on my domain, and never
take other liberties than such as I am quite
sure they have a right to take. Even while I gave
the greeting, the wife of my guest came briskly
in, and I was soon on good terms with both the new-
comers. The woman of this household was very
soberly attired, and, I noticed, wore her suit of
brown without any appearance of dissatisfaction.
The birds have among their many gifts some that in-
struct the preacher. They are preachers, and I am
never more at home than when I get the sermon of
their preaching So far as I have discovered, the
sermon sticks to the text, and the text to the sermon. All the sermons of my bird parishioners read
and sound like that of St. Paul, that "women adorn
themselves in modest apparel." At all events, that
is the instruction of the every day pulpit of life among
this great host, and while the men wear the "outward adorning," it is their teaching that they walk
among their fellows as though they had it not.
From both parties, however, the one parable after

9

all, that the gifts are talents to be used rightly, else no going forward into the fullness of life.

Pardon the digression, kind reader. Purple crowned and his modest wife knew nothing of it, and so perhaps will go on, all the better preachers. They stayed long enough with me, however, to illustrate some of the very best of bird activity. They are workmen in the great vineyard that " needeth not to be ashamed." Occasionally the head of this little household would open some of the simple strains of his quiet melody, and I fancied that the apple blossoms had " ears to hear." Does the effort of the singer heighten the color of the raiment he wears ?

Some way, among the birds the song seems to be closely allied to the beauty which flashes in the brilliant hues of the singers' attire. The purple crowned sparrow lifts his head, opens wide his little throat, and as the notes ripple forth, the neck and back glow in the changing purple hues as though some invisible Raphael was drawing his most brilliant lines. Now and then it seemed as though the bird knew that the song and the beauty were the proclamation from his housetop, and that it was his right to be it, in the honest pride of the bird's heart. But surely he had too much good bird sense to let any such matter do him much harm. Almost ever day he tells out the gladness of his heart in song, and when I am listening, seems a little overconscious of the effort.

The nest was hung in one of the smaller trees of the old cemetery, a snug little house lined with sparrow like neatness, and a home of quiet bird life that I found myself watching with increasing interest until the little family moved into the wider house that scarcely knows the boundary wall. While I write I notice the tenth nest building by robin hands on the rectory grounds, double the number I have ever known in one season before.

XVII.

Forty years ago a bird was common in all our pastures which I scarcely meet at all now. Its local name is mirrored in the single note which it utters rapidly when disturbed. Every school boy knows the kildeer, and something of its habits. Its haunts are the swampy ground of the open reaches extending along the low places of the pastures or meadows. Some way it seems the most restless of our many birds. At the least alarm it rushes away into the upper air, winging its rapid course with no perceptible effort. Where other birds deem a short flight all sufficient, the kildeer passes high into the air and hardly pauses until out of sight. Its trim body seems to balance perfectly on its broad, strong wings, and I remember, as a boy, I used to entertain the idea that the bird's incessant cry of kildeer helped it on its way. In maturer years the notion grew into almost a certainty, for I never saw the flight without the stimulus of the cry. I know of no other small bird whose flight seems so much a mere gliding through the air. As I see it, there is only at wide intervals any movement of the wings, and then it appears like a stroke that is hardly needed. If I should write all my thought, I should say that the great bird pasture of the air opened its arms to this bird and bore it onward and upward as a part of its very self. How this bird ever is satisfied to make its house on the ground and take up patiently the housekeeper's duties, is one of the problems of bird life.

But it is not much of a house, so I suppose the duties are not very exacting. A little depression somewhere between the tufts of grass is all there is of the nest. It contains usually four cream white eggs. The nestlings, like young partridges, run nimbly into the grass as soon as hatched. Their raiment is a soft fluffy down and to the eye they appear at a little distance like a puffball of creamy hue that has just sprung up out of the earth. The parent birds are unremitting in their care and in a short time graduate the little fellows as first-class navigators of the birds' ocean home.

Another familiar bird closely allied to the kildeer is the sand piper, or, as it is sometimes termed, the tip-up. In early June this bird appears, having made the long journey from its far winter home in the tropics. Almost every little pond throughout our entire state is allowed at least one family of these

busy fellows, while the streams are peopled at every
turn with some member of the great host.   I know
of no other bird that is so nearly an illustration of
"perpetual motion " as this little sand piper.   He
is never still in his wakeful moments. I have watched
him for many minutes at a time and never saw him
for an instant without the little piping note, and with
each emission of sound there came the up and down
movement of the body which gives him his local
name of tip-up.   One of my most vivid recollections
of the spring lot on the old farm is closely associated
with piper's curious ways.   His children were the
wonder of our boyhood days.   Many a time the
cows came home a little late, and the boy when
questioned of the tardiness, confessed that the lost
time was given to an interview with the little pipers,
which seemed to call to him out of the sweetflag, a
step or two down the sluggish stream from the old
spring pond.   The nest, like that of kildeer's, is built
apparently without trying and is of no use particularly
after the young are hatched.   I have a notion that
some of the animals which make their home along
the water courses secure a majority of the water
birds' young. The activity of the mink places him
first as a thoroughly equipped hunter, and of course
he gets the lion's share.

Another bird which frequents the low places of the

fields and swamps is the woodcock. It has a high reputation among sportsmen as a game bird, and epicures regard its flesh as one of the richest delicacies of the table If its quiet be undisturbed it will pass the day at rest. At the first signal of twilight, however, it begins its noctural rambles. Its foraging is peculiar. I have seen the soft mould punctured with holes, every inch examined closely and made to yield its quota to the bird's support. With the deepening of the darkness I have often heard the bird winging his way to the upland, where he could search the corn fields perhaps all the night through. The flight is rapid and at times accompanied by a whistling sound which seems to have a little touch of song in it.

I have never seen the nest, but from the habits of the bird I should conclude that in simplicity it rivaled those previously noted in this paper. The snipe, as I know him, is closely related to the woodcock. He gives us a little of his time in the spring and autumn, but finds his nesting place in the far north. The hunters enjoy his visits and usually manage to levy large tribute on his more or less crowded ranks. With the woodcock and the pipers he flies away to the far south for his winter home. All the birds named in this paper are practically songless. They have their single notes varying in length and loud-

ness, but no consecutive song like the field sparrow
or the bobolink. They are also attired in the soberest raiment that the birds wear. There is no perceptible difference in the plumage of the sexes. I
wonder a little why these citizens of the marshes are
denied these cheery things. Some of their fellows,
like the marsh sparrow, sing with rare melody, but I
do not now recall a single species dwelling in the
damp reaches of our fields, that wears in any degree
the raiment of brilliant colors. Two or three reasons
are easily uncovered why this is wise. Essentially
these are all birds of the ground. They nest there,
find their food there, and rarely alight anywhere else.
Bright colored plumage would increase largely the
danger from their many enemies, while the attractive
song might be a new peril in the same way. It may
be that in their own vernacular they sing and know
the song. Carlyle says: "The deepest thing in
man is song." Why not the bird made like that, at
home, to his own ever a song?

But however it may be, touching the singer and his
song, our birds of the marshes have one accomplish-
ment that puts them quite first among their fellows.
They might well bear all of the deprivation men-
tioned to be the accomplished runners they are.
Over the wet sand, hard and firm, they pass with flying feet. I have seen the young of both the kildeer

and the piper dart through the tall grass so quickly that one could hardly detect more than a little ball in rapid motion. Frequently the sand bars of our smaller streams seem to be a sort of bird stadium, and diminutive pipers the runners, the great trees and smaller shrubs-the audience of solemn mien and judgment, never warped by the least taint of favoritism.

XVIII.

One species of our native birds has entirely disappeared from New York. In the far west I believe there are a few left, but in a short time they too, will yield to the will of the sportsman, and the wild or passenger pigeon become a thing of the past. The last that I saw was a small flock in the wilds of Oklahoma. Fifteen years have passed since then, and I apprehend the bird is not now found east of the Rocky Mountains. The annual flights of these birds 40 years ago were the events of the year. The spring flight began usually in April, and for a week or more the great flocks passed in almost unbroken succession. In the autumn, after the young birds had attained full size, the second flight of the season occurred. The autumn flight was almost always the larger, and continued for a greater length of time. In 1840 I remember the fall movement was unusually large. At times the sun was sensibly darkened by the immense flocks. It became quite a problem with the farmers how to protect their wheat fields from the depredations of the birds. The writer well remembers being placed as a mere boy in one part of the field, while the grain was gathered at another point, and even then large numbers of the pigeons would swoop down and appropriate much more than their share. All the o'd fowling pieces and muskets in the country were brought into requisition without sensibly lessening the numbers, while thousands were netted and killed in other ways.   Soon after the first frosts the birds slowly disappeared, and, curiously enough, still kept their close fellowship.   Somewhere at the west or southwest they established, as by common consent, their winter home.

Here immense numbers would assemble and spend the nights, scattering during the day time far and wide in search of food.   I believe one of the last pigeon roosts of any size was in the southern part of Indian Territory.   Here in the evening the birds would assemble daily, crowding in on the branches of the great trees until they broke under the weight in every direction.   The hunters gathered from all parts of the country, and the daily slaughter was many thousands.   The wild flesh eating animals came thronging to the feast, and the wonder was that a bird remained to tell the tale.   A few years, however, of this wholesale destruction practically exterminated the species.

Their nesting was a counterpart to the roosting.

A tract of forest trees would be so densely occupied that every available spot would hold a nest. Frequently the trees would break and fall under the strain, until when the nesting season was over, acres of forest would be almost utterly ruined. These places of assembly were long distances from the feeding grounds of the birds—sometimes a hundred miles and more. The wild pigeon's marvelous power of flight enabled it to range in a single day the territory of one of our largest states. Hence their gregarious habits did not in the least interfere with the supply of food. The nest of the pigeon is a rude structure of sticks and grass that hardly deserves the name of nest. Usually the young are two in number, and grow so rapidly that they are soon ready for the life on the wing. This bird has no song, but utters a number of low notes, some of which are sounds that seem to be almost the soft breathing of the great trees. One can but regret that a bird of so many attractive qualities should entirely disappear from our midst. I see no way, however, by which he could have been preserved.

As the country was settled and improved the wild pigeon in the very nature of the case would disappear. The compensation largely is in the multiplying of the song birds, and with such an exchange we may well rest content.

Another of our birds which frequently reminds me
of the wild pigeon is the common cuckoo. As he
flies directly from one and alights, the movement is
almost an exact counterpart of that of the pigeon.
We have several varieties of the cuckoo, but the yel-
low-billed species is the most common. The English
cuckoo has a clouded reputation from the fact that it
deposits its eggs in the nests of other birds, and
leaves to them the task of rearing its young. Our
bird has been charged with the same practice, and
doubtless is not entirely clear of the charge. I have
no personal knowledge of any instance of such impo-
sition, but several of our naturalists aver that it does
occur.

Early this season the cuckoos appeared in the
rectory yard, and I soon knew, by the daily visits,
that two families were domiciled somewhere near.
Ten days later one pair disappeared, so I knew that
their home was broken up. The other pair continued, and a little later the low chuckles from beyond
the church told me that the young family was on
the wing. For a few days they interviewed me frequently, then went out into the wider world for the
long vacation. Later in the fall they may look in
upon me for a few days as they pass to their winter
home. The cuckoo comes to us late in the spring,
and usually leaves for the south early in the fall.

10

Perhaps it is true of him that he comes the latest and goes the earliest of all our birds. His song, if such it can be termed, never seems at the best only on the hottest of the summer days. It is essentially tropical in sound, and seems not only to break out, but to be broken with heat. Its nest is usually given a place in some thicket a few feet from the ground, and the bird's passage to and fro through the branches is a cheery lesson in graceful gliding motion. To some the abrupt notes of the cuckoo seem sobered with melancholy. To them his advent is not hailed with delight, and the nesting near the house portends more or less misfortune.

Like some of the other birds, he is credited with the gift of foresight. His rain song is well known in all the country side, and I am disposed to think is regarded with more favor than that of any other bird. I cannot detect any difference in the notes he utters just previous to a shower, and the ordinary song in the clearest day. Very likely all there is of the foresight is the quickening of life in the atmospheric changes which precede the approaching storm.

I notice the cuckoo is not a favorite with the other birds. For some reason they seem to cherish a pronounced antipathy to this sleek summer visitor, so I infer, without ever having seen the act, that the cuckoo is guilty of the charge of robbing his fellow

birds' nests. That he does it with the best in-
tentions I have no doubt, but that would not by any
means save him from the hearty dislike of the ones
thus summarily deprived of their own. His work
among the worms and insects is a redeeming quality
which accords him a worthy place among the farmers' best friends.

XIX.

I do not now recall a season when the kingbirds, or giant flycatchers, have been so plentiful as they are this year. They have nested in nearly every orchard and little grove of the parish. The young are now out of the nest, and I meet them in large numbers everywhere, in field and at the roadside. I am quite sure the kingbird rears his family without much disturbance. I know of no bird that ventures to assault the kingbird's stronghold, and surely there is no member of the feathered family that this little fellow fears in the least. He stands guard over his household, and any other bird designedly, or carelessly approaching it, is met far out from the threshold with the most vigorous kind of opposition. I think he delights in an opponent of large size. He seems to learn very quickly that the smaller and more active party in the contest has the advantage. At any rate he moves to the attack on the larger bird with a certain enthusiasm that does not appear when the antagonist is of lesser size. So far as I know, with a single exception, there is no bird of the air that really battles with any heart against the kingbird. He is king in his realm.

That such a condition should yield many tyrants is a foregone conclusion. I think I have seen attacks made by this bird that had no basis, only delight in the exercise of power. Last week I was witness to a scene of this character. A little bevy of crows had dropped down into an old pasture and were busy feasting upon the swarming grasshoppers, when a kingbird from a neighboring orchard discovered the happy flock. He sallied out immediately and apparently without the least provocation, gave battle single handed, to the entire flock of crows. At the first note of the enemy's bugle, the crows, in their slow, measured way, lumbered off to the neighboring wood. There was not the least sign of any defense, but the retreat was not rapid enough to save the black fellows from heavy strokes. With that peculiarly sharp, ringing note, the kingbird flashed above the crows and dropping upon them, gave blow after blow, only desisting when the wood was reached. The whole scene had its ludicrous side, and one could hardly yield much sympathy to the retreating crows, when perhaps a little courage on their part would have repelled the diminutive antagonist. He attacks the hawks in the same bold manner and, I am told, does not hesitate to assault

the eagle if the king of birds encroaches on flycatchers's domain.   Some one has written that the purple
martin, a bird about the kingbird's size, often gets
the best of him and that the battle. is frequently
joined between them and fought so fiercely that it
ends in the death of one of the combatants.

The nest of the bird is snugly made and lined
with no little skill.   The number of children varies,
but usually four are hatched and reared.   Flies of
all kinds form the principal diet of our bird, but he
is not at all averse to a change in the daily routine.
At times he has a pronounced relish for the honey
bee and frequently needs some sharp lessons to pre-
vent serious loss to the bee keeper.   Some kinds of
fruit are also found on his table, but his principal
work is done among the flies, so that he may be always ranked as one of the farmers' best friends.   The
extent of the country over which he roams is very
large, reaching from Texas to Canada, and, it is
said, as far west as the Rocky Mountains.

His cousins among our feathered friends are
numerous.   The great crested flycatcher, the wood-
pewee, the phœbe bird and the little flycatcher are
the principal ones.   Of these the most familar is the
phœbe bird.   Almost every farmhouse has its pair
of phœbes.   Its single note, sounding like the word
phœbe, rapidly spoken, gives the bird its local name,

while its quiet domestic tastes endear it to all lovers of home.   One peculiarity of the phœbe bird is that it returns to the same nesting place year after year. At the old farm house in the years agone, a nest was built in the woodshed just over the door, where the many members of the family passed to and fro daily.   For ten years and more the nest was built annually, and the young birds reared.   Probably some nestling of this family returned in the later years, and the habit was only changed by the removal of the nesting place.

The little flycatcher that appears in our yards and orchards, has some of the prominent traits of his kindred.   He nests annually near the house, and is quite satisfied to use for the purpose of house-building almost any kind of materials.   A family of these birds domiciled in my apple tree, and I never saw a busier household   Flycatching went on daily until the young birds were hatched, and then it seemed as though it went on night and day.   Sitting in my study I could hear the snapping of the bills, and I had my relish for the feast with the birds, for each fly was freebooter in my vineyard.   The wood-pewee of this family is to me the sad singer of all our birds. His pensive note is the minor strain of the forest, and when he is at his summer resort it can be heard at almost all hours of the day.

All the members of the flycatching family dress in the somberest brown, and in general form have little of the beauty of other birds. Little or no song is vouchsafed them. Still they have their compensation in certain traits of character that distinguish them among their many fellows. With valor flawless, they illustrate the type of bird character which provokes to the good work of high courage. Some one has said that he knows " that the Bible is inspired because it inspires him." I think we all know that kingbird, and the members of his kind, are stout-hearted, because they make us stout-hearted

Their song is the music of the valorous deed and that always is the rich melody of the gods. With the advancing season I note the changes in the habits of my large bird parish. To-day, the 6th of August, the swallows and the bobolinks are gathered in large flocks, preparatory to their long journey to the winter playground. Nearly all the birds are now bidding adieu to the settled home life, and while they drop some things that have endeared them to us in many ways, they take up and illustrate some new traits that impart an added interest to our study. They are now free lances in the wide realm of birddom, and with a new gladness tell the story of God's revelations among that legion of creatures, one of which does not fall to the ground without his knowledge.

XX.

In our closing article, it remains to gather some
of the straws that seem to have scattered by the way
Quite a number of our birds are yet so much on the
wing that we have only given them very slight notice
in passing. They will keep, however, until we have.
opportunity to serve them on some other occasion.
Bird nature is peculiar as well as perfect, after its
kind. It conforms strictly to the old gospel maxim,
"Take no thought for the morrow." It is with
birds now as ever, no laying by in store, no reaping
and gathering into barns, but the feeding in the
great store-house of nature—the Heavenly Father's
open hand. I do not know of one of our native
birds that hoards a store of food. They all feast
and enjoy, and as a rule sit at a well-spread table.
The birds' means of rapid movement enables him to
levy tribute on a wide extent of country. Most of
them may easily, if they choose to do so, dine in a
different state every day of the year, while several
species may take each meal hundreds of miles apart.
The bird of the widest range is not easily discov-

ered.   Probably some member of the great water-
fowl family stands first in this particular.   Many of
them undoubtedly reach the pole in their northern
flight and push far down into the tropics for their
winter outing.   Of the smaller birds. the swallow
reaches a wide range.   But perhaps it belongs to
the diminutive members of the kingdom to cover
the larger territory.   The little humming bird,
I think. visits every part of the continent
where there is the least development of summer life.
The moment blossoms appear anywhere in the frozen
north. this child of the tropics flashes in and is perfectly at home.   If he so elects, he may take the
" wings of the morning" and remain in the utter-
most parts of the north, at eventide hieing again to
his morning haunts. just simply refreshed in all the
multitude of his labors.   For the form material, this
little fellow illustrates almost the practical annihila-
tion of space.   In the bird's feasting, he levies tribute on the food of the world.   The sweets of the
flowers, the insects of the air, the innumerable eggs
of the insects, the seeds of all the plants. are ever at
his command.   Such a thing as dearth of food is not
a part of the birds' usual experience.   One of the
marvelous provisions for this great family is found at
the glacier's side.   The Arctic summer comes in as
it were in a day.   The plants spring the flowers

bloom, insect life is abundant. Mosquitoes swarm
everywhere. All the larger animals betake themselves to the mountains, but the birds' paradise is
ready for its glad occupants. Several of our smaller
insect eating birds take possession of this ideal home
immediately. For themselves, and for their young,
food is most abundant, while immunity is secured
from many enemies through the very agency which
supplies the food. One of our most beautiful sparrows (the white throated) is found in this happy
company. In another direction, also, this storehouse
of the north ministers to the wants of the feathered
kingdom. The young of the mosquito spend their
first days of life in the water. During the short Arctic summer they literally swarm in the bays and
ponds, even with the water very cold from the fast
melting snow and ice. Millions of fish here find
their food, which in turn furnish food to the innumerable water fowl that throng this entire region during
the nesting season. In our own favored state the
place of the birds in the economy of nature is being
slowly recognized. The old notion that some are
helpful and some pernicious is largely a thing of the
past. Now we know that each species has its place,
and plays its own important part in the affairs of time.
Public sentiment has so far crystalized in the right
direction that nearly all our birds are now protected

by law, and the time is not far distant when we shall
include the few, so far outlawed. When all are thus
protected and the law generally honored, we shall
know many of our birds better than we now do, and
I am sure the character of a few of the species will
change largely for the better. In our papers we have
written little of the song with which they greet the
opening day. The counterpart of the early greeting
comes again in the evening, but not so clear and full as
in the morning. Fresh from the night's sleep and rest,
the bird is at his best, and there seems to be at this
hour a sort of generous competition which adds great
zest to the occasion. The matins of the birds open
when the first ray of light streaks the eastern sky. I
have a notion that some of the kinds sleep with at
least one eye open. In our latitude the robin is the
pioneer. The waking and the song seem to be one
with him. The first note is a clear ringing cheer to
the morning. It wakes all the sleeping echoes of
the groves and meadows. It is followed quickly by
another note, but ere a half dozen are sounded, the
birds of the district are all awake. Each sings his
own song, and each is at his best. The music flows
from its thousand rills into a wide river of melody.
The discord of the concert is a part we would not
lose. There are no discords in nature. Her songs
may break upon human ears in a medley of sounds

that seem at times a mere jangle of chords ; but to
him who hears aright there is only the harmony born
of the skies in it all. I have sat with listening ear
waiting for the morning song of the birds. From
the great hill nearly a mile away, I have heard the
faint notes of the hymn as the hill received the first
faint gleams of the coming day. Down the hillside
to the glades of the swamp the song rippled, a thousand voices vieing together, and there the thrushes
and jays, and blackcaps, and warblers joined in the
refrain, until the verge of the marsh would pass it on
up the acclivity to the rectory door, born anew every
step in the sweetness and joy of vesper, lark, and
bobolink. Someway it would seem to linger for a
moment with the one waiting for it, and then flow
away westward, enriched at every turn with new
voices. but ever the same glad hymn of praise.
What else is it so much as the processional which
precedes and heralds the day, its winged choristers
wonderfully suggestive of that other choir which in
its " holy, holy, holy," ceases not night nor day.
And so it is the morning song of the birds begins,
continues and knows no end. Every moment somewhere it is waning and waxing, too. What we get
in its coming and going, somebody gets somewhere
at each successive moment of time. " Old Eng-
land's drum beat " goes with it, but it is only here

and there on the line of longitude that the reveille of Britain is sounded. That of the birds outruns the lines of nations, fills all the lines and flows round and round the earth, its one great anthem of ceaseless praise. Ah, I can but write in closing what visions of the new day are here! What broad glimpses of the " city four square," its streets of gold, its tearless eyes, its unvexed harmony, its everlasting peace ! The winged creatures of God sing and give praise with the best member they have. To walk in the midst of it with open heart, is to catch the spirit that glows in the poet's words :

>   " Those ancient teachers never dumb,
>   In nature's unhoused Lyceum."

INDEX.